Don't Cry Over Spilled Potions

Which Village, Volume 3

L.C. Mortimer

Published by L.C. Mortimer, 2022.

DON'T CRY OVER SPILLED POTIONS

First edition. July 2, 2022.

Written by L.C. Mortimer.

Also by L.C. Mortimer

Which Village
Don't Cry Over Spilled Potions

Standalone
Swords of Darkness
Just Another Day in the Zombie Apocalypse
The Death of Planet 86

Just Another Day in the Zombie Apocalypse

Don't Cry Over Spilled Potions
L.C. Mortimer

For fans of Buffy, Charmed, and Hocus Pocus comes a story about second chances and new beginnings.

Don't cry over spilled potions.

Once upon a time, I was in love.

My husband was stolen from me before I was ready, but I found him again.

Now he's back.

He's here with me in Which Village, but he has no memory of the past and no idea that the two of us were inseparable.

When a foe from his werewolf days threatens to tear us apart, Stanley and I have a choice to make, and it's not going to be an easy one.

Don't Cry Over Spilled Potions is the third book in the WHICH VILLAGE series. This book features female main characters who are middle-aged (or fast approaching it) and who have magical powers.

For everyone who has ever dared to dream.

Chapter 1

Jaden

"Your mother is dead."

Those words are all it took to change my life.

In the blink of an eye, everything changed.

Everything I thought I knew was stolen from me.

Ripped away.

Everything I *loved* was taken.

Captured.

And I *broke*.

The pain took me, consuming me.

And then, over time, I realized that things weren't as terrible as I thought.

Hi.

I'm Jaden.

And I'm a witch.

I live in Which Village: the most beautiful town in the world. Most of my days are spent making potions and trying to perform magical spells, but my nights are spent with Stanley: my husband I thought *died*.

Well, he didn't die.

He lived.

Only, he kind of forgot about everything that made him *Stanley*.

And now we're here.

When he came back to me, I thought that everything was going to be okay. I definitely figured that the two of us were going to pick up where we left off, so to speak, but things have been awkward and...

Well, things have been uncomfortable for both of us.

And I'm not the only person who noticed that tension.

"What are we supposed to do about him?" Eliza asked one night. Stanley was upstairs sleeping while Eliza and I were sitting on the front porch drinking tea.

The two of us did this a lot: drank tea. We got together and made things happen. Sometimes a good ol' cup of tea could work miracles, in my opinion.

Right now, though, the answers weren't coming to me the way that they usually did.

I didn't know.

I didn't *know* what we were supposed to do about him.

It had been months since Stanley had returned to me, but he'd barely spoken during that time. I'd figured that a few days or *maybe* a few weeks would go by before the two of us were able to talk about what had happened to him, but I hadn't expected months.

And to be honest, I was feeling a little lost.

Stanley was the light of my life once upon a time. If I was being honest, he still was. He was still the person I loved more than anything and he was the one person I knew I could always count on.

Only, he was different now.

Quieter.

Sadder.

He'd been through something traumatic, and I didn't really know what I was supposed to do about it. I'd been through my own pain, so I knew that the world could hurt, but this was different.

I'd lost my husband, but he'd lost *himself*.

All of the memories that the two of us had made were gone.

All of the hopes and dreams and desires he'd had once upon a time had simply disappeared.

Now Stanley knew who he was because of what I told him, but I knew that it wasn't the same.

I knew it wasn't the same as being able to remember for yourself.

"He's been through a lot," I reminded Eliza gently.

The older witch nodded and sipped her tea. We were drinking iced tea from canning jars, which probably wasn't the most mature way to take our tea, but it was comfortable and relaxing, and those were two things I could deal with today.

"I'm aware."

"Healing wounds like these can take time," I added, but I wasn't sure whether I was trying to convince Eliza or myself.

"It's been months, Jaden."

"I know."

And the problem wasn't that I hadn't tried.

I'd been trying to find an answer to what had cursed Stanley. My mother had tried, too. Before she died, she'd been working to find a cure for the werewolf curse that held him captive.

Werewolves were turned when they were bitten by another werewolf. They couldn't control their ability to shift.

Shapeshifters, who were born and *not* made, were able to have full control over their abilities.

In some ways, I was jealous of them. I often wished I could turn into something else – someone else – and just slip away unnoticed.

My mother had known about these differences, too.

She'd been working on a potion that was supposed to be able to offer Stanley the ability to control his shapeshifting. With her potion, he was supposed to be able to turn into a wolf when he wanted and back into a human when he wanted.

There would be no depending on the moon.

There would be no relying on the night.

She'd *almost* done it, but then she'd been killed.

Mom had been too young, and she'd been taken far too soon. Eliza and I both missed her dearly, but I was still trying to take my sadness and pour it into solving the mystery my mother had left for me.

Now it was my turn to pick up where she'd left off.

"I can find a cure, Eliza," I told her.

I believed in myself. I believed in my mother, too. Her research, coupled with my sheer determination, meant that I was *going* to make this thing happen.

I just had to.

Eliza, however, didn't seem quite as confident as I did.

"You don't have a lot of time."

I looked over at her. The older woman who had loved my mother so dearly was staring off into the distance. She wasn't making eye contact, which meant that whatever she was talking about was actually pretty bad.

"Meaning?"

"Meaning that if you don't find out soon, he's going to be stuck in his werewolf form forever."

Chapter 2

Jaden

"What are you talking about?" I stared at Eliza, searching her eyes for clues. "I have *no* idea what you mean."

This was the first time I'd heard her say *anything* like this, and to be honest, I wasn't really sure that I was prepared for this sort of news.

I felt like I'd only just gotten Stanley back.

I didn't want to lose him again.

I especially didn't want to lose him to something like this.

"The curse of the werewolves," Eliza said firmly. Her hands gripped her canning jar full of tea just a little bit tighter. She said this like it was something I should have already known.

But I didn't.

There were a lot of things I didn't know.

And honestly, I was starting to get a little tired of that.

Once upon a time, I'd felt like I was doing just fine on my own. I was surviving. I was staying strong. Alive. Brave.

Now, every day was a struggle, and sometimes, I wondered if it had been worth it.

I knew that wasn't the best sort of thought to be having, and I knew that no matter what came next, I was going to have to make some hard choices.

I'd start now, with figuring out what Eliza was talking about.

Once she revealed whatever this secret was, I'd have to make a choice.

Would I keep trying?

Or would I give up?

"You're going to have to start from the beginning. Try to remember that I'm not a witch who has been around a long time."

In fact, *all* of my witchiness I had developed since coming to Which Village. There was a lot to learn about being a magical being, and I'd done my best to make sure that I was worthy of the name *witch*.

I didn't want to let down my mother's memory, but I also didn't want to let down the people around me.

So, I tried my best.

My mother had been an incredible part of the town, and I knew that her memory and her honor were two of the most important things here.

I didn't like the idea that someone might meet me, her daughter, and feel like I wasn't everything my mother had been.

Nobody wanted to let down the people they loved.

Least of all, me.

Eliza sighed. She shifted nervously on the top step, wiggling for a moment. Eliza was the best witch I knew, and it was easy to see why my mother had loved her. The two of them had been inseparable until the day my mother passed away.

Now, Eliza kept my mother's memory alive in many different ways. One of those ways was by doing what she was doing now. She was giving me a chance to feel like I had a mother again.

A guide.

Someone to look after me.

Eliza could never replace my mom, but she was a wonderful role model.

I was certain most people didn't consider 35-year-olds as worthy of role models, but I liked having one.

There was a lot to learn about being a witch and I honestly didn't think I'd be able to do it on my own.

"It's complicated."

"Eliza, I have nothing but time."

"Okay," she said slowly.

Something in my voice must have convinced her because she didn't argue with me nearly as much as I expected her to.

"Tell me."

"The curse of the werewolves is a nasty one."

"I figured that much."

From what I could tell, Stanley had lost most of his memories. He hadn't recognized me when he'd seen me for the first time. While he hadn't tried to run away, but he was a shell of who he'd been *before*.

Stanley didn't really remember that the two of us had been married. He didn't remember that we'd been in love. We could carry on a conversation, sure, but only about the vaguest of topics.

Most of the time, he retreated after a short chat. He'd head up to his bedroom and stay in there the rest of the night. Sometimes I heard him talking to himself, but most of the time, he was quiet.

Lonely.

Isolated.

Maybe he was scared.

I knew that I was.

I wanted my husband back, and I was starting to think I might never actually get that. I *needed* him. I needed him to be here for me. I needed Stanley to be the bold, wonderful man I knew he could be, and I needed him to fight.

Because I couldn't lose him again.

I wouldn't.

"Once someone is bitten, they lose a little bit of themselves," Eliza continued slowly.

"Their memories."

"More than that," she nodded. "Their hopes."

"That makes sense, I suppose."

These were things we'd talked about before.

Nothing we were talking about really surprised me.

"The thing about werewolves is that the more they turn into a wolf, the more they become comfortable in that form."

That would explain a little about what happened to Stanley when he'd come to me at the fair.

He'd been stuck in his werewolf form for a very, very long time. From what I could tell, it had started after my mother passed away. He hadn't come out.

"But werewolves can't control their abilities," I reminded Eliza. "Unlike shapeshifters, who can switch back and forth between a human and a wolf form, werewolves can't do that."

"Maybe not," Eliza nodded, "but after a certain amount of time, werewolves become emotionally satisfied in their werewolf form, and their body seems to catch onto that. They don't change back to their human forms even after the moon is gone."

"What do you mean?"

"Nobody bothers them when they're a wolf."

Nobody pesters them.

Nobody talks to them.

People just run away and leave them in isolation.

That's what she means.

"Are you trying to tell me that Stanley isn't going to keep changing back to his human form after the full moons end?"

She nodded. "Eventually, he'll stay. When that happens, he'll be completely wild. He'll run off into the woods, most likely, and you'll never see him again."

Eliza spoke bluntly, but I could tell that she meant well. I knew that there was a lot of good in her heart as she told me this.

That didn't make it any easier to hear, though.

"Any recommendations?"

Aside from what we were already doing, which was *everything*.

When I had free time, I used it to read about werewolves. I read my mom's journals back to front. I tried to talk to Stanley, but he just grew more and more sad.

I never thought I'd find my husband, only to realize that the carefree man I'd loved was gone and had been replaced by a werewolf with depression.

Not that I loved him less.

I loved him just as much.

Maybe even more.

The Stanley I knew now needed me.

Needed my help.

And I was going to give it to him.

I'd do whatever it took, I knew, to reclaim my husband and find the man he used to be.

But I needed a cure.

And I needed it fast.

Chapter 3

Fiona

I'd lived next to Alicia up until her death and now I lived next to her daughter, Jaden. I was a good neighbor, for all intents and purposes, but there was more to being a good neighbor than just not causing drama.

Being a good neighbor also meant paying attention when there were things people didn't want you to know.

There was a reason that neighborhood watches were so popular. People liked knowing they were safe, and they liked knowing that the people around them were going to protect them at all costs.

So, being a good neighbor meant protecting the people around you.

And sometimes, being a good neighbor sometimes meant lying.

So, when Jaden had asked me if Stanley had ever left the house without her, I'd said no.

I'd lied.

Because the reality was that the werewolf that she called a husband had, in fact, been sneaking out every damn night and walking away without so much a glance over his shoulder.

Instead of snitching on him to his wife and getting him in trouble, I'd done what any good neighbor would do.

I'd followed him.

The first night, I'd been surprised to discover that he was able to lose me rather quickly.

For a werewolf, he was a speedy sort of fellow.

Okay, interesting.

Where was he going?

What was so important that he had to go out on his own?

And why wasn't he willing to tell his wife about it?

That was what I really wanted to know. There was a reason he hadn't told sweet Jaden he was leaving.

Was he going out to do wolfish things?

Or was there something else?

I knew that he wasn't going to meet another woman. That wasn't something you could just *do* in Which Village. We were all too connected, too close to one another.

Besides, I saw the way that Stanley looked at Jaden.

She might not believe it anymore, but I knew without a doubt in my damn mind that he was crazy about her.

He just couldn't remember their history.

The next night, I'd followed Stanley again, but it had been much of the same. I'd managed to follow him somewhat discreetly for a few blocks, but then he'd slipped down a side alley I hadn't been anticipating, and when I'd reached it, he'd been gone.

Okay, so good for him.

He was a sneaky man.

The third night he left the house, I followed him for a longer period of time. I'd stayed on his tail until he'd rounded the corner, walked down a narrow street, and headed for a bridge.

I'd lurked in the shadows as he stood on the bridge that overlooked Weston's Creek. It was a well-known tourist attraction in our town. It was the kind of place where kids would spend their summers jumping off bridges.

It was the kind of place where magic happened.

Only, Stanley didn't look like he felt the world was very magical.

If anything, he seemed sad and disappointed.

He stood there, gripping the rail that overlooked the water, and he stared at it.

What was going through this man's mind?

And why was he so desperate to be alone?

After what felt like an eternity, he spoke. He didn't look over, but he didn't have to. I knew he was talking to me.

"Why are you following me?"

His words seemed to carry in the night.

At first, I was silent. I didn't want to answer. Didn't want to acknowledge the fact that I was there.

Then, when he turned, I could see it in his eyes.

Yeah, he meant me.

He wanted to know what I was doing bothering him.

And he wanted to know why I wouldn't leave him alone.

He'd noticed me sticking with him, and he wasn't a fan.

Okay, well, too bad. Maybe I wasn't a fan of him hurting my neighbor. Jaden had been quite sad since he'd arrived. She was his *wife*. She was supposed to feel happy and excited, but she hadn't.

Instead, she'd spent a lot of time crying and not a lot of time baking.

I didn't want to be a grouch, but she hadn't baked cookies for me in weeks, and I quite missed that.

Baking, even as a witch, was something you had to feel good in order to do. It was like magic. If you were sad or upset, your magic spells were going to be sloppy and imprecise. It was going to be harder to get anything done at all.

Staying where I was, I didn't answer at first.

Then the werewolf turned toward me. He raised an eyebrow. He was still in his human form, but that didn't change what he was. And it certainly didn't change the way I saw him.

Stanley, in my opinion, was more than a wolf, but he'd been trapped in his werewolf body for so long that it had changed him in some ways.

He straightened up, standing a bit taller.

"I'm talking to you, witch."

I stepped out of the shadows and frowned at him. I didn't like the fact that when he said this to me, it almost sounded like a slur.

Was I a witch?

Yes.

Did I like it when he used that tone of voice with me?

Absolutely not.

"Excuse me, young man. I don't appreciate you speaking to me like that."

Who the heck did this person think he was?

Oh, sure, he was the husband of a witch. Who cared? A lot of people were married to witches, and none of them gave me a hard time the way this man was.

"I'm sure you know who I am."

"You're Stanley," I said. I put my hands on my hips and hoped I looked intimidating. "Why are you out here?"

"It's a nice evening to go for a walk."

I glanced up at the moon without meaning to. When I looked back and met his eyes, they were sad.

"I'm safe tonight," he told me. "No werewolf stuff." Stanley held out his hands, just to prove his point. His skin was smooth and soft.

Human.

He didn't have the fur that he would grow once the moon decided to change his form into something else.

Something scarier.

"I didn't think you were going to," I said gently.

He stared at me for a long time before he turned back to the water in front of him. He placed his hands on the railing of the bridge, and then he took a deep breath.

"You're afraid of me."

"No," I shook my head.

"It's okay. A lot of people are."

"I'm not."

"Really?" Stanley turned and looked at me. He raised an eyebrow. "No offense, Fiona, but why should I believe you?"

"Because," I said, pushing my shoulders back.

For just a moment, I wondered if I should tell him. I probably should have, but when I saw his eyes, I knew that Stanley needed something that I could actually offer him.

He needed hope.

And I had that in droves because I knew that there was hope for him to still have a life despite what had happened to him.

"My mother was a werewolf."

Chapter 4

Jaden

Years ago, when Stanley and I first got married, we loved to travel. One time, we took an incredible trip to Seattle that was supposed to only be for a weekend, but that somehow turned into two weeks of coffee shops and exploring.

We stayed in the world's coziest little hostel and spent our days sipping coffee and reading books.

It had been heavenly.

And then it had been over.

When we'd returned home, we'd talked about going back again. Instead of visiting Seattle a second time, though, we'd explored other parts of the world. We'd gone anywhere our hearts desired, and it had been everything we'd ever wanted it to be.

And we'd had so many adventures.

So many wonderful experiences.

One of my favorite memories was the time we were in a coffee shop in Tokyo, and I'd been laughing about the weather. We'd tried to time our trip perfectly so that we'd avoid rain, yet it had somehow rained almost every day of our trip. I had found it ironic, but Stanley hadn't cared at all.

He'd hauled me into the street, coffee in hand and everything, and he'd danced with me there.

He'd kissed me even though we were both totally soaked, and he'd promised to love me forever.

I'd promised him right back.

And I'd meant it.

There were so many memories bouncing around in my head that I wanted to share with him. There were so many little pieces of my heart that made up our life together that it felt impossible to separate them up. I couldn't divide our relationship into "good memories" and "bad memories."

There were just *our* memories.

I wanted to ask him if he remembered the time that we went into a coffee shop we thought looked cute only to find that it was secretly a karaoke bar. We'd ended up staying long into the night just singing our hearts out.

Or there was the time we'd tried to find a local zoo but had accidentally ended up in someone's backyard petting their pet cows. The farmers had politely asked us to leave, but they'd had a good laugh with us first.

There were so many wonderful, crazy experiences that the two of us had enjoyed together, but they were over now.

And I was starting to wonder if I needed to give up on the idea that he was ever going to be the Stanley I had once loved.

Or if he was ever going to remember.

This man before me at the breakfast table wasn't the man who had once adored me.

This man could barely look at me.

And every single day, as I searched and searched for some sort of cure, I wondered if he was ever going to look at me the way he once had.

Was he ever going to adore me again?

Was he ever going to want me again?

I didn't want to be pathetic or weak, but I missed him. I'd said goodbye to him when he'd "died." I'd moved on, or at least I thought I'd moved on.

Only now, I wondered if it was ever really going to be over between the two of us.

Now I wondered if we were ever going to make it happen for us again.

"So," I said, sipping my coffee. I was gripping my mug far too tightly. I was going to break it if I wasn't careful, but for some reason, holding onto my cup was the only thing I felt like I was in control of.

Since when did things between us feel awkward and forced?

They *never* had before.

Never.

If anything, our relationship had always been so wildly calm and relaxing that people had teased us about it.

Now we were like strangers.

"So," Stanley said. He, too, had a cup of coffee in front of him, along with a piece of buttered toast that he hadn't eaten. He'd made it, and he'd buttered it, but he had yet to actually bring it to his mouth.

I'd noticed that Stanley didn't eat very much anymore. I wasn't sure if it was because being a werewolf had diminished his appetite or if it was because being around me made him feel nauseous and uncomfortable.

I wasn't sure which would be better.

"What did you read about last night?" I asked him, desperately fishing for *anything* to say. He'd gone to bed early, still sleeping in the guest room, and he'd been quite intent on the fact that he wanted to read.

"I read a zombie book," he told me. "Lots of killing. Lots of zombies. I think there was even a werewolf in chapter six." Stanley raised an eyebrow when he said this.

Was he messing with me?

"Really?"

"No."

"Oh."

Yes, he'd been messing with me.

I stared at him, but when he looked up at caught me, I glanced back down at my coffee. I hated how uncomfortable I felt around him now.

After all I'd been through to find Stanley, I wished beyond everything else that the two of us could make this work.

All I knew for sure was that if I didn't find a cure soon, I was going to lose him forever, and it might not be because he turned into a wolf.

It might be because now the two of us were strangers and neither one of us knew how to push past this and find what we'd lost.

I finally brought my mug to my lips, finished my cup of coffee, and got up to leave the kitchen.

I couldn't deal with this any longer.

Chapter 5

Fiona

There was a knock at my door mid-morning, and I pulled the door open to see Stanley standing there. He was wearing a button-down shirt with a pair of loose-fitting jeans. His hands were shoved in his pockets.

Stanley looked more like a middle-school boy than a middle-aged man. I considered him for a moment.

"Stanley?"

What was he doing here?

I knew him, sure, but he didn't belong here anymore than Jasper did.

Then again, nothing seemed to stop the damn cat shapeshifter from coming around. I wasn't really sure how I'd managed to acquire a shapeshifting cat for myself, yet I had.

"I want to talk."

"About what?"

"Your mother," he told me.

Of course.

I stared at him for some time. There was a part of me that wondered whether I should actually let him in or not, but the truth was that he looked so damn pathetic I knew that I needed to.

Stanley wasn't here because he wanted to chit chat or catch up on what I'd been doing for the past few months. He wasn't here because he knew it was going to be Christmas soon or because he had some great ideas for the town bakery.

Nope.

He was here because he was feeling alone, and I was probably the only person who could help.

After all, it wasn't like many werewolves had children.

"Come in," I told him with a sigh. "I'll put the kettle on."

*

Three cups of tea and eight cookies later, Stanley was ready to listen to what I had to say. Up until that point, he'd just been sipping tea and snacking, but he finally pushed his mug away and looked up at me.

"Please, Fiona. What can you tell me?"

A lot: probably more than he wanted.

"What do you want to know?"

"Everything," he said. "Everything and anything. I think that anything would help."

"And why is that?" I wasn't really in the habit of talking about my childhood or my upbringing. My parents were strange people and even though I loved them, I couldn't *really* say that I missed them. Not in the way I was supposed to.

Having a werewolf mother hadn't been easy, but we'd somehow found a way to make it work.

Somehow.

"Because I don't know what to do. I don't know how to talk to my wife anymore. She looks at me like I'm a freak and I hate it."

And that was the real problem, wasn't it?

It was never about being a werewolf. It was never about Jaden's new witchy powers. It was all about their relationship and how it had changed. It had broken.

He wanted it back, and that was probably never going to happen.

At least, even if the two of them managed to make things work, it wouldn't be the same. I could tell that just by looking at him.

Still, even if their relationship had scars when this was all over, he was wrong about something.

"I don't think she looks at you like you're a freak," I pointed out. I couldn't imagine that Jaden would do that.

Only, it didn't matter.

Did it?

It didn't matter if she did or didn't do that. What mattered was that Stanley *felt* like she did, so to him, it was practically true. No matter what Jaden said, no matter what she wanted him to believe, it was all irrelevant if it didn't match his feelings.

"I feel like she's afraid of me," Stanley whispered.

"Have you talked to her about that?"

I already knew the answer before he shook his head.

Of course, he hadn't. Talking about your feelings was never exactly an easy feat.

"It might help."

Stanley shook his head, though, and brought the conversation back around to where he wanted it to be.

"Tell me about your mother."

I snapped my fingers and one of my books jumped off the shelf and floated through the air to the table. I didn't get to show off my magic much these days, so I was going to make the most of the moment. Stanley raised an eyebrow but didn't say anything.

"My mother was a beautiful woman," I said, opening the book to a page that held her picture.

Tall, lovely, strong: she was everything I'd always wanted to be. She'd been a witch, just like her mother, and her mother's mother. We were all witches.

And then she'd gone and gotten herself bitten, and everything had changed.

She'd still loved me, and she'd still cared for me, but being bitten meant that she was different.

"I can see that," Stanley nodded, looking at the picture. "Was she always a werewolf?"

"Not until I was a teenager. She went out on a trip and came back with a strange bite. The next full moon, we knew."

"So, what did you do?" Stanley wanted to know.

"Do? We didn't *do* anything. She was my mother, and she was a werewolf. That was that."

"And your father..."

"He accepted her," I told him. That was the best damn thing about my father. He hadn't been afraid, and he hadn't been scared. He'd just accepted Mom for who she was.

He'd just believed in her forever and always.

"I wish..." Stanley's eyes looked pained.

"Go talk to Jaden," I told him. "She will understand, Stanley, but she can't read minds."

I wished that Jaden could read minds. Wished that I could, too, to be honest. It would make my entire life *so* much easier.

"I don't want to talk to Jaden," he said sadly.

"She's the only one who can help you, Stanley," I said. "Give it a chance."

He stared at his hands for a long time and then he looked back up.

"She wants a cure. She wants to cure me and then she wants to love me, but Fiona, it's never going to happen. So, do you really think she can learn to love me even if I'm a werewolf forever?"

"This is Jaden we're talking about," I told him. "Give her a chance, Stanley. She's been through worse things."

"Somehow, I find that hard to believe."

"Then you don't know the Jaden that I do."

Chapter 6

Jaden

A few more days passed, but I still didn't have any answers.

I still didn't know exactly what I was supposed to do when it came to dealing with Stanley.

The reality was that to me, the man I'd left behind was still back there in the past.

The person in front of me was just...

A stranger.

"So," I asked, looking up at Stanley. He was still so handsome. He had big, beautiful eyes that seemed to sparkle. He was staying true to the Quartz name, as far as I was concerned.

I thought he was going to try to start some sort of awkward conversation, the way that we always did, but Stanley didn't. Instead, he went straight to the heart of the matter.

"You don't like me," Stanley said. "Do you?"

His voice was quiet. There was a bit of disappointment there. A little bit of sadness.

I like you," I told him.

More than that, I loved him. He was the one person I'd always been able to count on, and now I was being offered the chance for him to count on me.

The problem was that I felt like I was letting him down.

He'd been through so much. He'd gotten lost in the world, and he'd had to deal with that loss on his own. He'd never been able to find any sort of safety or compassion during that time because everything had been about survival.

"I'm just sorry I wasn't there for you," I told him.

Stanley cocked his head. This surprised him. Apparently, he didn't realize that I felt like I'd completely failed him.

"What? What are you talking about, Jaden?"

I hadn't been there for him when he'd needed me. I hadn't been around when he'd been lost in the world. Stanley had been forced to survive for *so* long without anyone by his side.

He had a wife.

I should have acted like one.

"You were all alone, and I really believed you were dead."

I shook my head. I was embarrassed.

I was ashamed.

I was disappointed in myself for believing that there was even a chance that he didn't want or need me.

The idea that he didn't *love* me never even came into play.

But I wondered if he himself felt unloved.

He'd been alone and lost, and my mother had somehow managed to find him before I did.

"Jaden, it's not your fault," he told me. "None of this is your fault."

"How can you be so sure?" I asked. "If it was me, you never would have stopped looking for me."

We both knew that much was true.

I sighed and shook my head.

There was this normal part of grieving where people denied the death had happened. I'd done that. I hadn't wanted to believe that Stanley was dead, so for a long time, I'd pretended like he wasn't.

Only, eventually, I'd had to move forward with my life.

Eventually, I'd had to keep going even though I didn't want to.

"What did you do when you realized I was gone?" Stanley asked. There was a hint of sadness mixed with curiosity.

I just looked at him.

What had I done?

I'd broken.

I'd cried.

I'd yelled at the universe and begged the world to bring him back.

I hadn't wanted to accept that the person I'd planned my entire future with wasn't going to be around to see that future.

"I missed you," I said quietly.

Stanley had been living in the house with me here in Which Village for a couple of months, but neither one of us had actually talked much. I had been so very happy that he made it here, and I'd been so very happy that he was wanting to be with me, but it wasn't really the same.

There was still something missing from all of this.

For some reason, this was our first time talking about what had happened. I'd been focused on trying to find a cure, and I thought that Stanley had sort of just been focused on trying to seem normal.

Well, nothing about this situation was *normal*.

Nothing about our relationship seemed like it was okay anymore.

"I missed you, too," he said to me.

He didn't have to say that, though.

I knew it was a lie.

"Stanley, we both know that isn't true."

"I didn't know it was you that I was missing," he told me. "I just knew that there was something."

"Do you remember coming here?"

"Which Village?"

I nodded. I knew that Stanley and my mother had been in contact in the year after his "death."

Neither one of them had bothered to tell me, of course, which hurt, but I probably shouldn't have been surprised.

My mother had managed to keep her witchiness from me for a very long time. If she hadn't gone and died, there was a chance I might never have known when I'd come into my powers. Honestly, I might have just lost them entirely.

Only, she had died, and I had come to Which Village, and I had learned all about who I was and who I was meant to be.

And Stanley had the unique experience of getting to know my mother in all her witchy wonder.

I hadn't.

"I'm not sure how I found my way here," he told me. "I can't really explain it. After everything happened, I got lost. I traveled for a little while, but not on purpose. I still can't remember what happened before I was bitten."

I'd read about that. For some people, being bitten by a werewolf was like being born a second time. It was like no matter what they did, they couldn't remember their life in the before time.

And I felt bad for him.

I felt sad for Stanley.

He'd been dealing with this for a very long time. He'd been struggling with the isolation and the loneliness. He'd been hurting.

And he'd been alone.

"How did you end up with my mom?"

That was the question I'd really been wanting to know. If he'd managed to get together with my mom, then something must have drawn him here.

Only, he shook his head.

"You don't know?" I asked. It's okay if you don't know."

If he didn't remember, then I couldn't really fault him for that. Could I?

Here was a man I had loved for just about a million years. There was nothing Stanley could do to make me stop loving him.

Even if he no longer felt the same way about me, I would still love him.

"I don't know what led me to your mom," he said. "There was just something about this place. It's like it has an aura about it.

"What do you mean?"

"I think it has to do with the fact that the moon was charmed," he shrugged. "I know it was designed to lure werewolves out of hiding, but it definitely worked."

He's talking about the former mayor who did her best to make this place a nightmare for all of the werewolves in the area.

They didn't exactly have a lot of say in how things worked. They couldn't just not become werewolves when there was a full moon.

"Your mom recognized me," he said slowly.

"What do you mean?"

"I came here on a full moon night, but I found my way to her house. She didn't seem surprised. I think it's because you share her blood. I think I was looking for you."

So, maybe he didn't hate me.

Maybe he didn't dislike me as much as I feared that he did.

Maybe he was just sad.

Lonely.

Scared.

And maybe he was afraid that he wasn't going to get his memories back.

"My mother couldn't find a cure," I said gently.

A statement, not a question.

She was so close to finding it. If she succeeded, then her work died with her.

Stanley looked at me carefully.

"You remind me of your mom, you know."

There was a sad part of myself that wished my mom reminded him of me.

I was the one who had known him first.

I was the one who had gotten to know him personally.

And I was the one who had loved him.

Above everything else, I had loved him so, so much.

I didn't complain, though. Instead, I just tried to appreciate the fact that he was here, and he was with me, and so far, nothing had gone wrong aside from the fact that he couldn't remember.

"What did you and my mom talk about?"

"Mostly you," he admitted.

"Me?" Why me?

"Your mom was really proud of you," he told me. "She was always talking about you and your work.

Now that, I could believe. My mother had always been a very proud sort of mama bear.

It was one of the things I missed most about her. No matter what I was going through, I'd always been able to call her if I really needed to.

Not that I'd talked to her in the years leading up to her death. The two of us had grown apart in many ways, but it was nice to know that she'd helped my husband.

She'd done her part to save the man I loved.

That had to count for something.

"Did she ever talk to you about her search for answers?"

He nodded. "All the time. Those books you have upstairs? She spent all of her free time with her nose buried in them."

"You remember the books?"

"I remember everything that happened after I was bitten. I just can't remember anything before."

That was good to know, though. Maybe it could help. Maybe that could be the secret to unlocking all of this.

"You know, Fiona's mother was a werewolf."

I stared at him.

"Um, no! I did *not* know that."

How the hell had I been living next to Fiona for so long without knowing that very important information?

He nodded.

"Her parents stayed together even after she was bitten. Fiona's mom was changed when Fiona was already a teenager. Kind of crazy. She stayed with her husband, though. They lived a relatively normal life until their deaths."

I stared at him. "That's possible?" She was able to lead a normal life. How could she have led a normal life?

She was a *werewolf*.

She'd been a werewolf, but she had still had a husband and a kid.

"I don't know," Stanley said. "It's something to know, though."

"Stanley," I said, leaning forward. I placed my elbows on the table even though I knew perfectly well that it wasn't good manners. Nobody liked when someone put their elbows on the table. There I was, though: doing it.

"Jaden?"

I bit my lip for just a moment before I blurted out the question that had been concerning me. I wasn't just looking for a cure, after all. I was also trying to protect Stanley from anything that might come after him.

After us.

"Fiona was concerned that you might have made...enemies."

I wasn't really sure how else to put it.

Werewolves had a lot of enemies. Even people who didn't *know* werewolves hated them. It was actually one of the things I felt worst about.

Nobody deserved to be hated by the people around them, yet werewolves always seemed to get the short end of the stick.

People had this idea that werewolves were dangerous and unfriendly and mean.

They thought they were cruel.

They weren't, though.

At least, Stanley wasn't.

During the months he'd lived with me, he'd changed into a werewolf a couple of times. He'd asked if I wanted to lock him up in a cage the way people always did in movies, but I thought that was inhumane.

He couldn't control *changing* into a werewolf, but Stanley didn't seem to have any problems controlling himself once he was in his werewolf form.

"Yes, I'm aware that she's concerned about this," he said.

I stared at Stanley. When I'd first met him, his hair had been long and shaggy. He'd looked like a rockstar, in my opinion. I'd always thought that of him.

Now, it still sort-of looked that way.

During the first part of our marriage, he'd cut his hair and kept it short, but now it was long and flowing, and it reminded me of a simpler time.

It reminded me of a time when everything seemed like it was going to be okay.

It reminded me of a time when I didn't feel quite so alone.

"Is there anything I should know?"

He sighed. Shook his head. Looked at his hands.

Nice try.

"I've known you longer than you think," I pointed out. "And I know that there's something you aren't telling me."

"Oh? You know that, do you?"

I nodded.

"What is it? Is someone after you?" What I really wanted to know was if they were going to come *here*.

Were they going to come after our new life?

Were they going to come after us?

And would my magic be enough to stop them?

Chapter 7

Jasper

Being a shapeshifter wasn't all bad, in my opinion. There were plenty of perks and things that worked out well for me.

For example, I got lots of pets and lots of snacks. People were always happy to feed a "stray." Sure, I was anything *but* a stray cat, but nobody seemed to care.

I'd been shacking up at Fiona's for some time now, and I could sense that I was nearing the end of my welcome. Eventually, she was going to want me to leave her alone and get my own place.

Sooner or later, she was going to insist that I do something like move on from her living room couch.

I didn't want to, though.

I liked staying at Fiona's.

I liked Which Village.

I couldn't guarantee that everyone in town liked me back, but it was a nice place filled with magic and a little bit of mayhem and mystery. It was enough for a shifter like me. It was enough to keep me happy.

I was getting better at blending in, too. The more I practiced, the more I came across as a real cat. It had many advantages, in my opinion.

The biggest?

People *talked* around animals.

It was easy to assume that people would bite their tongues when cats were around, but that wasn't actually the case.

Instead, people gabbed.

They shared secrets.

Stories.

Mysteries.

There wasn't much that people wouldn't say around a nice cat like me, and that was how I learned a lot of information.

I learned about the sales and who was having trouble with their magic.

I got to find out who was going on vacation and where.

I even got to hear the gossip about everyone's non-magical relatives.

And of course, I also found out that there was a newcomer in town, and nobody knew who he was.

But he was very, very curious about werewolves.

It was after Stanley had already left Fiona's for the day. The two of them had shared this long heart-to-heart that, while touching, had also been pretty cheesy.

It wasn't really my style.

Fiona had talked about her parents and Stanley had expressed that he missed his.

It had been a big ol' thing, and I was glad when it ended, and he finally left.

Only, Fiona chastised me for eavesdropping and kicked me out of the house until supper time.

Now it was past dinner time, but I hadn't gone back just yet. It was late, and I was tired, but I knew that it was better to go back later, rather than sooner.

Fiona didn't exactly have a lot of patience these days.

Since I was in my cat form when she booted me out, I didn't have clothes to change into, so I had to stay as a cat all day. Now, even with the darkness of night starting to settle around me, I hadn't changed back.

This wasn't the worst thing in the world, of course.

Being a cat meant I could nap where I pleased, and it meant I could climb trees without looking crazy. Nobody wanted to peer out of their own window and see a grown-ass man walking around naked, so I stayed in my cat form.

That was how I saw the man crawling toward Jaden's house.

At first, I thought I was seeing things. I didn't really trust my eyes.

Then I looked a little closer and realized that there was, in fact, a man creeping closer.

An enemy, perhaps.

Or maybe someone who was lost.

Only, if someone was lost, why would they be sneaking around near the bushes?

Why would they be using the cover of darkness to do as they pleased?

There was a part of me that knew no matter what was going on right now, it wasn't my business.

Only, there was a different part of me that was unwilling to accept that.

This was my business.

This whole place was my business.

Everything about this place...

It was my business.

My home.

My everything.

When I'd first come to Which Village, it hadn't been a place I expected to stay, but I was here now, and I didn't plan on going anywhere.

Jaden and I weren't exactly close.

We weren't besties.

To be honest, we really weren't even friends, but I knew that in spite of everything else, I couldn't let her be the person who got hurt because nobody stopped the villain.

I meowed loudly, but nothing happened.

The man glanced over and turned back toward the house, where he kept prowling about. He alternated between crawling and crouching as he moved along, but finally, he stood up, and I could see that he had a collection of supplies with him, as well as a bag of some sort.

Was he a robber?

A burglar?

Or was he one of these enemies-from-the-past that Fiona had worried about?

I meowed at him loudly, catching his attention, and the man seemed to be completely caught off-guard by this.

He seemed to trip, all of a sudden, and his bag went flying. He gasped, shocked, as his bag hit the ground. Then he turned and started running.

Why was he running?

I was just a little cat.

That was when the first explosion sounded.

Chapter 8

Jaden

I felt the crash before I heard it.

An explosion.

A burning.

Stanley and I had been sitting in the kitchen when it happened, and I stopped breathing for a moment as my mind tried to register what was happening.

Then I reacted with magic before I even turned to see if Stanley was okay because I really, really didn't know if he was okay. The explosion and crashing was so loud that it shook the entire house, and then things started breaking.

The roof was splintering off and the kitchen now seemed to be on fire. One of the cabinets fell off the wall, clattering to the floor. My tea set, which had been displayed on the counter, shattered into a million pieces.

And all I could think about was Stanley.

I was worried about him. I needed to make sure that he wasn't hurt and that he hadn't been injured, but the reality was that Stanley was just as strong, if not stronger than me.

And he knew a lot.

He knew about surviving because he'd done it for so long.

And he knew what to do when there was danger. My magic sent a small bubble around Stanley and me, enclosing us and the kitchen table all I one small space.

It was a protective ball that would keep out the fire and prevent boards and nails and shards of glass from hitting us.

All around us, my house seemed to be going up in flames.

So much for rebuilding, I thought glumly. I'd only recently finished rebuilding after my mother's old house had burned down. Now I wondered if it was even going to be worth it. Perhaps I should have known better than to build on the same land Mom had owned.

"What's going on?" I yelled to Stanley.

I wondered if Fiona had been right.

Had someone been trying to get Stanley?

And were they coming after me now?

"I don't know," he yelled back. "But we need to go."

He couldn't move because of the bubble. It basically locked us in place.

My house was falling down all around us. Something had hit it or damaged it. I wasn't really sure. The ceiling seemed to be crumbling inward on itself, though, and it didn't look like there was anything that was were going to be able to do about that.

The chaos had been set in motion.

"Let's just get out of here," Stanley called out to me.

Only, there wasn't any way for us to do that. I didn't know how long I could hold the barrier around us in place. Already, I could feel myself weakening. I wasn't a particularly strong witch.

Wasn't very brave.

Didn't have a lot going for me except for the fact that I had finally, after so much time, finally found my husband.

It felt like we had been apart for an eternity. It felt like we'd been losing ourselves slowly over so many years. Now, though, we were bac. We had this. We were making it happen.

And we were really going to let a little thing like blowing up be the thing that destroyed us.

No.

No, we weren't.

"How long can you hold that for?" Stanley asked.

"Not much longer. Maybe a few minutes." Although, if I was being honest, probably not even that long I was already so tired and worn out that I was afraid I was going to lose myself - and that I was going to lose us - if I didn't keep this thing going.

It was impossible to tell how much time we had left. "Can you get us toward the door?"

I looked toward the kitchen door. It led directly to the backyard. We were only a few feet away. Stanley and I had been sitting at the breakfast table, but honestly, if we moved carefully, then yes, I could get us there.

I was almost completely certain.

"Let's do it, Jaden. We need to get going."

Stanley looked worried, but when our eyes locked, I knew it wasn't just because of the house crumbling down around us. There was something else, too. He was afraid of whoever had done this.

And I was almost certain that Stanley knew exactly who they were.

Chapter 9

Stanley

I thought I was going to be safe.

At no point had I anticipated that the two of us weren't going to be able to make this thing work.

"Jaden, we have to go."

It seemed like time stood still as the two of us slowly made our way toward the door. A moment later, when we reached the doorframe, I nodded at Jaden.

At the same time, she let go of the boundary she'd created for us, I reached out, turned the knob of the door, and pushed it open. We leapt through just as the house collapsed in on itself.

We'd done it.

We'd survived.

My heart was pounding a Jaden and I fell onto the ground. I reached for her hand and squeezed. It didn't matter that I had no memories of the two of us together.

What mattered was that I knew the two of us were meant to be together. I knew it in my heart. The two of us were supposed to be mates forever.

And I could feel it.

I could feel the connection between us.

It didn't matter that so much time had passed. It didn't matter that I wasn't sure what we were supposed to do. It didn't even matter that I felt so lost and broken without her.

The only thing that mattered was that we were together.

We were together, and I was going to do everything in my power to keep it that way.

But first, I had to get her somewhere safe.

I had to protect her.

We couldn't stay here. Not with someone lurking in the darkness who wanted to catch us. Instead, I reached for her hand, hauled Jaden to her feet, and tugged.

"Come on, baby," I called as we started moving. "Let's get out of here."

Chapter 10

Jaden

He took me to a cave.

I wasn't sure why I was surprised, but I was. Although Which Village was actually located on the edge of a mountain, I didn't really spend a lot of time thinking about how there were mountainous caves nearby.

And I certainly didn't spend a lot of time thinking about how I would feel being alone in a cave with him again.

Stanley looked at the cave like it was a place he knew, like it was a place we'd be safe.

That was what we needed.

Ever since he'd come to live with me, things between us had been awkward and tense. I hadn't really expected them to get better or more comfortable, but I found myself missing what we'd been before.

There wasn't passion between Stanley and me anymore, but it was more than that.

It was like our friendship had faded, too.

Now, I found myself standing on the brink of something new. I was facing a major choice.

I could go forward, or I could leave.

I could move on with him, or I could run away.

I didn't want to go back to where I'd been before.

And I didn't really want to leave.

I stared at the cave and looked over at him. For a moment, I was worried that I was going to do something stupid.

Like kiss him.

Like try to pretend that things were the same as they had been so many years ago.

We were running from whoever had destroyed my house, but more than that, we were running from our pasts.

We were running from whatever secrets were lurking in his, especially.

Finally, I spoke up.

"What is this place?"

We were standing at the entrance to the cave. I wasn't really sure if I wanted to go in or not. There wasn't really anything particularly remarkable about the cave. It was just some place.

It wasn't like it was a place we could stay forever.

Although honestly, it didn't look like a place where anyone stayed at all.

Maybe ever.

"A place I know."

"How do you know this place?"

"I come here sometimes."

I stared at him.

"When it's a full moon?"

"Yes."

"So, this is like, your werewolf hideaway."

"Something like that," he nodded.

So, he was letting me in.

He was letting me see exactly what he'd been up to.

He was sharing his secrets with me.

And I liked it.

I felt a rush of confidence and happiness wash over me as I realized what was going on.

He was letting me into his world and helping me survive at the same time. I wasn't going to take this lightly. Not at all.

But first things first: I wasn't a shapeshifter.

I wasn't a werewolf.

I couldn't see in the dark.

Whatever was chasing us wasn't going to stop just because we wanted them to. They'd keep coming, and we needed to be ready.

We needed to be prepared for whatever was coming our way.

"Can you see in there?"

"Yes."

Of course, he would be able to see in the darkness. Maybe being a werewolf had its perks. Still, I was going to need *something* if I was going to go sneaking around in spooky caves.

"Do you have any torches or lanterns?"

"No."

Once upon a time, Stanley had been a man of few words. It seemed as though that hadn't really changed. Now, just as then, he didn't have a whole lot to say to fill the space between us, but that was okay.

I was different now.

I was older.

I wouldn't say I was wiser now, but I did know a lot of things that I hadn't known before.

Like magic.

I hadn't known magic.

Now, I flicked my thumbs and a small ball of light appeared before me. It was no larger than a quarter, but it glowed brightly. I pushed it forward, sending it into the cave where it hovered in the center of the room.

"How'd you do that?" Stanley asked, looking at it.

"A lot of practice," I muttered. More practice than I wanted to admit. Although I'd been a witch for some time now, I didn't want to admit that I still wasn't very good at it.

The more I tried to make things work for me, the harder it seemed to be.

I thought that magic was supposed to get easier, but so far, it definitely hadn't.

From what people had told me of my mother, it sounded like she was good at magic: an excellent witch. It seemed like no matter what she did, everything always fell into place for her.

With me, things were hard. I had to work twice as hard at everything I did just to make my magic *sort-of* okay.

Still, Stanley seemed impressed, and a thrill shot through me.

He was proud of me.

"What else can you do?" Stanley asked, looking at me. He hadn't seen me do a lot of magic before. Although he'd been in my house and I really should have tried more, our relationship had been something we were both a little uncomfortable with.

"What? With the cave?"

He nodded.

"I don't know. Clear out the spiders?"

There were definitely spiders in a cave like this. Probably, there were a lot of them.

While tiny monsters didn't scare me. I'd never really been their biggest fan.

"Let's see."

Oh, he wanted more?

I could give him more.

A wave of my hand and a couple of carefully whispered words sent a group of spiders scurrying in all directions. Some of them ran toward us, but Stanley and I each stepped back to let the steady line of tiny arachnids through.

He looked up at me once they had passed, and he shook his head.

"You amaze me, Jaden," he said.

Then he walked into the cave, leaving me staring at him.

Had I heard him correctly?

Had Stanley really just said I *amaze* him?

My heart swelled as I clung to his words.

Maybe everything really was going to be okay, after all.

Chapter 11

Jasper

Fiona stared at me.

"What's wrong with you?"

"I'm hurt," I told her. "Someone bopped me on the head."

"Who?"

"I didn't see him clearly," I told her. "He was at Jaden's. He's the one who blew up the house."

"I can see that," Fiona said.

She was standing in the window by the open curtains, looking at the firetrucks that were sitting in front of Jaden's house. Even though Which Village was a small, magical sort of place, there were still firetrucks and people who did their best to make the town seem safer.

I wasn't sure if it was a magical explosion or if this was Alicia 2.0, but the firefighters were doing their best to get things under control.

"Alicia's place was blown up," Fiona said.

"I'm aware."

"And someone has done the same to her daughter's place."

"Yep."

"It's a mystery."

I stared at Fiona.

"It's not really a mystery."

"Oh, but it is." Fiona clapped her hands. She was *excited*, I realized. It wasn't often that she had excitement in her life anymore, but this...this was something incredible to her.

"Fiona, it's not a mystery," I insisted.

"Look, Jasper, what do you know? You're just a cat."

My jaw dropped. "Just a cat? Seriously? That hurts, Fiona. Really, it does."

"You know what I mean," she waved her hand.

"I'm afraid that I don't, actually."

I'd been called a lot of names in my life, and I'd been given a very hard time for being a shapeshifter, but I'd never been called *just* a cat.

Ever.

Until now.

I bristled, irritated. I wasn't offended on a personal level, but on a friendship one.

Fiona was supposed to be my *friend.*

Friends didn't use the word "just" when talking to each other.

"You don't know what you're talking about," I glared.

She just shrugged and waved her hands around. On cue, her pots and pans started floating around the kitchen. Spices, herbs, and ingredients followed, ready to mix together into something that was hopefully even *slightly* edible.

The last thing I needed was to have a rough day and then not be able to even eat.

"Fiona, who do you think it was?" I asked as she stepped away from the window. I took her spot as a watcher, looking out over all of the cars and vehicles that were lined up on the street.

I saw Eliza step out of a dark green truck a moment later and start surveying the damage. Once upon a time, she'd been in love with Jaden's mother, Alicia.

That had been a long time ago.

Even though it had been just over a year, I was certain that it felt like longer in some ways.

It probably felt like a damn lifetime ago.

"I don't know," Fiona said.

"Eliza's here."

"What?"

Fiona marched over to the window, pushed me out of the way, and peered outside just in time to see Eliza glance over at us. Her eyes narrowed when she realized that the two of us were watching.

I promptly shapeshifted into a cat.

"Seriously?" Fiona asked, staring down at me.

I couldn't talk in my cat form, but yes, I was serious. I wasn't about to face Eliza in my human form. Not when I knew what she was going to say.

I leapt up into the air and landed on the counter.

"You can't leave me alone with her," Fiona whined, but I was already jumping up to the top of her cabinets. I landed easily and then flattened my body up there. When Eliza came in, she wouldn't spot me.

At least, not right away.

Who knew what she'd do when she realized I was eavesdropping?

Eliza wasn't the type of person I wanted to upset on a good day. Today she was going to be even more annoyed that someone had blown up Jaden's house and that Jaden was now missing.

A second later, we heard banging on the door.

Eliza had come over, and she was – as suspected – in something of a mood.

"Ugh," Fiona groaned. She sat down at the table and waved her hand. Her ingredients kept flying around and mixing together. She was going to finish her recipe no matter what, apparently, and I had to respect her for that.

"Let me in!"

"It's unlocked," Fiona muttered under her breath.

It was either loud enough for Eliza to hear or the witch simply decided to turn the knob because Eliza marched into the room, slammed the door behind her, and looked right at me. She didn't even look at Fiona! She went right for me.

"Cat! Where the hell is Jaden?"

I stared at her, blinking.

How the hell was I supposed to know?

Chapter 12

Jaden

Stanley led me to the back of the now spider-free cave. The cave itself was small – probably the size of a little living room.

"We can't stay here for long," I pointed out. "They'll definitely find us."

I still didn't know who *they* were.

"There's a hidden door," he mumbled, gesturing to the bottom of the wall. There were a couple of large rocks there that, sure enough, seemed to be concealing a small crevice that was *barely* big enough for a person to crawl through.

"You can't be serious."

"We can crawl through."

"I'm not crawling through there," I said firmly.

He looked at me, staring.

"But there are no spiders," he said.

"I'm still not doing it."

I couldn't.

I couldn't go through such a small, little space. It just wasn't going to happen.

Stanley might have been brave, but I wasn't.

Not anymore, and not in a place like this.

I didn't want to crawl through there.

"Hey," he reached for me and pulled me close so that our bodies were touching. I was pressed up against him tightly.

Once upon a time, this gesture would have made me feel safe.

To be honest, it still made me feel safe.

It was like a warm reminder that I was his, and that he was mine, and that the two of us had something really special together.

Only, that had been a long time ago.

"It's going to be okay," Stanley told me.

Somehow, and for some reason, I had a feeling that he meant about more than just the cave thing.

He didn't just mean I was going to be okay crawling through that little crevice.

He meant I was going to be okay with him.

With us.

"Stanley, I'm trying so hard to find you a cure," I told him.

I was so certain that if I could figure out what my mom had been working on, then everything would be okay.

If I could just figure it all out, things would be fine.

I could get my husband back to normal and he'd get his memories back and then...

What?

What would happen then?

It had still been two years since I'd lost him.

I was still so different from the girl he'd left behind.

After Stanley died – or I thought he died – I'd had to become strong.

I'd been forced to take care of myself in so many ways.

I'd had to do a lot of different things in order to survive, but mostly, I'd had to learn to live without him.

And it had been hard.

I was a stronger person now, but I wasn't that girl he left behind.

Only sometimes...

Sometimes I missed her.

Chapter 13

Stanley

I wasn't sure how I was going to tell her, but it was almost time.

Jaden had been strong for a very long time. Even though I couldn't remember her from *before*, I could tell just by looking at her that she had been a fighter.

After she'd lost her husband – me – she'd done a lot of things to keep herself in one piece.

She'd fought.

She'd toiled.

She'd worked her damn ass off.

And now she was still doing that.

She was still fighting every single day because she wanted me to live. She wanted me to be normal. She wanted her husband back.

Only, she was never going to get him.

"It's going to be okay," I told her again. "Let's get into the inner-part of the cavern, and then I'll explain everything."

"What do you mean, Stanley?"

"Let's just go."

I looked over my shoulder.

It was still dark outside, but the sun would be coming up in a few hours.

The sun would rise, and we'd go back home with the protection of daylight on our side, and then we'd keep moving forward no matter what that meant.

Right now, though, I needed to keep her safe.

"Get on your tummy and crawl through," I told her.

"How do I know this isn't a trick?"

"It's not a trick."

"How do I know you're not an imposter?"

"I'm not an imposter?"

"How do I know-"

Only, I'd had enough.

I couldn't take any more questions. I couldn't take any more arguing. I wasn't sure that my reaction was the best one in the world, but I grabbed Jaden by the shoulders, and I pulled her close. I pressed my lips to hers, and I just kissed her.

I kissed her like she was my everything because she was.

I kissed her like I remembered her even though I didn't.

I kissed her like she was a goddess because deep down inside of me, I knew that this was how I'd felt about her long ago.

When I pulled back, she stared at me for a long minute.

"You still don't remember me, do you?"

"No."

I didn't see a point in lying. I knew that it probably hurt her, but I couldn't lie to the woman I'd loved so deeply, once upon a time. I wasn't going to make her pay again and again in that way.

One round of heartache was enough.

"Okay," she said. "I'll go."

She got on her stomach, summoned another little light ball, sent it ahead of her, and started crawling.

Chapter 14

Jasper

It took a lot to calm Eliza down, but I was finally able to explain what I'd seen, what the man looked like, and what I thought was going to happen next. She didn't really believe me when I told her that I didn't know who it was or where they'd gone.

"But they're alive," she said.

"They're alive," Fiona agreed.

"Who could have done this?" Eliza asked.

"You're the mayor," I pointed out. "What do you think?"

It was an unfair question, but it held truth. Eliza had been running Which Village for some time, and she was the one person who knew the inner-workings of the entire place.

She knew who came into the village and she knew who left.

She knew who had enemies and she knew who didn't.

And she knew, most of all, that Stanley wasn't being honest about where he'd been since he "died."

"I think he's got an enemy," she said.

"That's what I said!" Fiona insisted. She turned to me and glared. "Didn't I say? I said that."

"She did, actually," I nodded. She'd said it a couple of times, actually, and it was starting to get pretty damn annoying having to hear how "right" she was all of the time.

"I just don't know who would want to hurt poor Stanley," Fiona sighed, shaking her head.

"It's not like we know that much about the guy."

Eliza considered this for a moment. Then she nodded.

"Jasper's right. We don't know very much about him at all."

Fiona gasped, as though she was somehow offended by this, but I didn't really get why.

"You know that we don't know very much about him. Why are you acting so shocked?"

"It's just that this... Well, it feels like Alicia should have been more open about all of this..."

Eliza clasped her hands together. I could tell she was trying to be kind of diplomatic, but it was hard for her.

After all, Alicia had been her girlfriend. The two of them had been wildly in love and they'd planned to spend the rest of their lives together. They just hadn't expected for "forever" to be such a short time.

"Alicia had plenty of secrets," Eliza said slowly.

That was when it hit me. Somehow, I hadn't realized it before.

Alicia hadn't told her, had she?

Stanley had come back to town and had spent a bunch of time with Alicia. I should know. I saw them sneaking around from time to time. Hell, people even thought I was the one who had killed Alicia because I resembled Stanley in so many ways.

Only, Eliza looked like she'd been dangerously betrayed.

And a betrayed woman wasn't a good one.

Not a good one at all.

Chapter 15

Jaden

"What happened?" I asked Stanley.

More importantly, why were we hiding in a cave?

The interior part of the cavern where we were hiding had obviously been used before by Stanley. There was a little mattress with a blanket and a pillow in one corner, and despite the fact that the space felt very, very damp, it wasn't the worst or most terrible place I'd ever been in my life.

I was starting to think that it was actually kind of a nice place.

It was actually kind of relaxing.

There was *nothing* here.

There were no cell phones.

No people.

Nothing to bother us.

For the first time, it felt like, Stanley and I were alone and free to do as we pleased.

We were free to do whatever we needed to.

And we could talk freely.

"I fought hard to get here," he told me.

"I know you did."

"Your mother helped me so much," he continued.

"So, what's the problem, Stanley? Why did someone blow the house up?"

"I'm not supposed to still be alive."

"Meaning what?"

"Meaning that there are other werewolves around Which Village."

I looked at him. I didn't really get what he was trying to tell me. Why would other werewolves in the county be a problem?

Why would they come after him?

"Stanley, you aren't making any sense."

"I invaded their space," he told me. "And I tried to look for a cure. The werewolves around here hate the witches. Me working with your mother was seen as a betrayal, especially to one werewolf in particular."

"Does he have a name?"

He looked at me and nodded.

"Yeah. His name is Joseph, and he'll do anything to stop me."

"Just because you were working with my mother?"

"It's more than that."

"It's not, though. Is it? You wanted a cure. He didn't. Why should that stop you from trying?"

I was starting to get frustrated and honestly, a little sad. I didn't want to think of Stanley having to fight any longer. I didn't want him to have a hard time anymore.

Perhaps most of all, I didn't want him to have to deal with the reality that some people didn't think he should get a say in how he existed.

If he didn't want to be a werewolf, Stanley should have the right to reject that and be a human again.

If he wanted to be with me, he should just be with me.

"Werewolves have been around for a long time, Jaden."

"I'm aware."

I'd spent the last year studying them, after all. I knew the habits of werewolves. I knew the kinds of places where they lived. I knew that some of them stayed in little hidey holes like this one.

I understood that for some wolves, life was a tricky thing.

For others, it was pure hedonistic indulging.

"Not all of them want to be freed from their prisons," he continued.

I closed my eyes for a moment, just thinking about what he'd said.

"And what about you?" I asked him.

"Excuse me?"

"Do you want to be freed?"

I was starting to think that Stanley didn't really want a cure as much as I did. There was a part of me that wondered why I still hadn't been able to find anything in my mother's work to indicate that there really was a solution to the problem.

I knew that my mom had been searching for a long time, and I knew that she'd been working with Stanley, but I hadn't found it.

Why hadn't I been able to find it?

If such a cure existed, and if she was *so* close to finding one, shouldn't I have known by now what I was dealing with?

Maybe Stanley didn't want to be cured.

Could there have been a part of him that wanted to stay in his werewolf form?

I could never understand what he was doing through. Maybe he liked the freedom he felt as a werewolf.

Maybe he liked the way he actually got to finally relax.

"It's not as simple as you think," he lowered his voice.

I thought he was going to say something else, but just then, we heard a howl. It was the loud, low, feral moan of an animal.

Or maybe of a wolf.

"Shhh," he whispered, pressing a finger to his lips.

The creature was here.

The person hunting us was almost here.

And we were out of time.

Chapter 16

Eliza

Where would they have gone?

That was perhaps the biggest question for me.

Where would they have gone, and why would they have gone there?

It wasn't a secret that both Stanley and Jaden were resourceful people.

Jaden, after all, had managed to go through mourning for both her husband and her mother, and she'd seemed to suffer no ill-effects for it.

At least, none that I was really aware of.

Had it taken her some time to get over losing her mom?

Yes.

Had it taken her a little while to learn to use her powers?

Of course.

But she'd done it.

And she'd basically done it alone.

I wasn't going to be the person who claimed to have all of the answers, but I did know that Jaden wasn't going to take whatever the problem was lying down.

She would fight because that was what Jaden did.

She was a fighter.

So, where would a fighter go?

I had to think of this from her perspective. I had known her for some time, but not just the last year.

I'd known Alicia much, much longer.

And as Jaden's mother, Alicia had valuable insight into her daughter.

To be honest, there were many things Alicia was tight-lipped about when it came to her child, but one thing I knew without a doubt was that Jaden was strong.

Brave.

Unstoppable.

No matter what she did, she gave it her all, and I guaranteed that was what she was doing now.

"Where would she go?" Fiona asked, voicing my question. I knew she couldn't read minds, but sometimes I did wonder.

"Somewhere quiet," Jasper muttered.

I look at him.

"Why?"

"What?"

"Why would she go somewhere quiet?"

He shrugged.

"No, that's a good answer. Tell me why you said it."

Perhaps I should have been less bossy, but I *had* been an attorney. Technically, I still practiced law from time to time, but my primary job was now keeping the city safe from anything that could hurt it.

Taking care of legal issues was the least of my priorities these days.

Still, old habits died hard, and it was difficult for me to keep my voice calm and collected when I was talking to Jasper.

He was a shapeshifter, so perhaps his perspective was a little different than mine was.

"I just mean that she's probably not like, you know..."

His voice trailed off, but I latched onto what he had said.

She *wasn't* the kind of person who liked loud spaces, and she wasn't the kind of person who wanted to run and ask for help.

If someone had come to her house and hurt her, damaging the house itself, she would have been upset, and she would have run.

He was right.

"Stanley has been living outside of Which Village for some time," Fiona pointed out.

"The last year at least, plus the year that Jaden thought he was dead," I murmured.

For a whole year, the woman I loved had been trying to find a cure for the fact that Stanley was a werewolf, but she hadn't been able to.

At least, not to my understanding.

But Stanley hadn't stayed at Alicia's house. He hadn't stayed with her, so where had he stayed?

And could that have been where they went now?

Jasper nodded.

"You think he took her to his werewolf house."

"I don't know that I'd call it a werewolf house," I murmured.

"You probably should," Fiona nodded.

"We need a tracking spell."

"Ask Natasha," Jasper pointed out. Jaden's other neighbor was notoriously good at spells. She was a clever witch who could do a lot more than many witches in town.

Natasha often sold herself short, but in my opinion, she was one of the most powerful witches in the village.

"She's out of town," I told them both. "Her cousin was hexed, and she's got to help her."

Fiona and Jaden both stared at me, blinking.

"For how long?"

Nobody knew. Her cousin had read a spell from a forbidden book and gotten herself hexed.

Personally, I thought it was a bit crazy to go around reading from books you knew nothing about, but then again, what did I know?

Ignoring their question, I shrugged.

"There are other witches who can perform tracking spells."

"Like who?"

"Like me," I said.

"You can track people?" Fiona cocked her head. "I didn't realize that."

"There's a lot about me you don't know, Fiona."

"Unlikely," she muttered. Then she turned around and started strutting away. "I'll get the cauldron. Then we'll get started."

Chapter 17

Jaden

I closed my eyes and held my breath.

I wished I knew a spell for pushing people away. If I could expand my barrier-building abilities and make that barrier invisible, we'd be set.

Only, I knew that wasn't going to happen because the man who had been hunting Stanley was right outside of the cave.

I could smell him.

I knew that Stanley could, too.

Stanley's nostrils flared. Even though we were in the interior portion of the cave, he could still smell the guy sneaking up on him, and Stanley looked…

Well, he looked afraid.

And my heart sank.

After all of this time, and after everything he'd been through, my sweet Stanley was *scared*.

He was worried.

He thought that whatever came next was going to hurt him.

And I *hated* that.

I didn't want Stanley to worry about a damn thing. I didn't want him to have to be afraid because I wasn't going to let anything hurt him this time.

He might have been alone after he turned into a werewolf, but he didn't have to be alone now.

Lovers fought for each other.

Always.

And even though he couldn't really remember me, and even though he was sure that he was going to have to do this alone, he wasn't.

I was going to protect Stanley no matter what it took.

The little ball of light that filled the tiny space where we were sitting seemed to pulse. My magic tended to do that. The pulsing of whatever I'd created matched my heartbeat, and right now, my heart was racing.

Stanley reached for my hand.

"How long did you live in this cave?" I whispered.

"Long enough."

"And what did you do here?"

He looked over at me. The cave wasn't very well furnished. There was a little mattress pad and I could see a few boxes of snacks – mostly trail mix and crackers – but aside from that, it was barren.

"I slept here."

"It looks like this is the type of place you could just sit and ponder, too," I told him.

He nodded.

"It's quiet here. Nobody comes this way. I was able to spend a lot of time just thinking about what I was supposed to do."

"Did my mom know about this place?"

Stanley shook his head.

"Nobody knew about this place, Jaden. Nobody but me."

I nodded. Sometimes it was nice to have a place that was all your own. That was how I'd felt when I'd finally finished building my house.

It was *mine*.

A feeling of satisfaction had wrapped around me once it was complete because I finally knew that I had a place of my own. I had a space where I could just be myself and nobody could come bother me unless I let them.

And I wasn't planning to let them.

That was what Stanley had here. He had this little fortress. He had a place where he could just be *himself.*

"Why trail mix, though?" I asked.

"Come again?"

"You were in your werewolf form for a long time after my mom passed away. Why would you keep these snacks here?"

"Werewolves still have to eat, Jaden."

I stared at him, blinking. I realized that I had never actually thought about what werewolves ate. For some reason, I'd always just assumed that they ate a lot of meat or that they hunted wild animals.

"And you like to eat trail mix?"

He nodded.

"Why?"

"It just makes me feel comfortable," he said quietly, and I realized that Stanley had spent a lot of time feeling very *not* comfortable.

Not anymore.

Once this was all over, I was going to do everything in my power to make him feel safe.

Secure.

And happy.

I wanted to make him feel happy.

Chapter 18

Stanley

Turning into a werewolf wasn't really what I expected.

Although, if I was being honest, I didn't really know what to expect.

There was a part of me that thought the entire thing was some sort of weird, cosmic joke.

Like, the universe had looked at everything the world had to offer and thought, "yep, this loser's a real clown. His life needs to be harder."

And that was it.

Now I was hiding in a cave with the woman of my absolute dreams, and I knew that no matter what came next, there was no return from this.

There was nothing I could do that would make this pain go away.

From here on out, I was destined to be sad.

And I did feel sad.

Jaden was beautiful and sweet, and even just judging from the time I'd known her recently, she was kind.

She'd taken me in when she didn't have to, and she'd *cared* for me.

She'd protected me.

But there was still a lot that Jaden didn't know.

"I have a comfort food, too," Jaden told me.

"Is it also trail mix?" I cracked a smile. She was adorable and she didn't even know it. I could tell that Jaden had once been soft and giggly and happy, but she was harder now.

There was a new strength to her that made her a bit rough around the edges, but she still had that gentle, gooey center.

She still wanted to be a good person.

She wanted to help people.

"No!"

"Well, don't leave me hanging."

She smirked. "Do you really want to know?"

"Of course."

"Raisins."

"I don't believe you," I told her.

"No, it's true."

"There's no chance that I would ever marry someone whose comfort food is raisins," I told her firmly.

She seemed to find this hilarious because she laughed again, but the howl from outside of the cave sounded once more.

This time, it was louder.

Closer.

Whoever was hunting us – whether it was Joseph or someone else – they were tracking my scent. They had to be.

That was the only explanation I had for how they could be growing closer and closer.

Besides, there was no full moon tonight. Whoever was coming after us might be a werewolf on most days, but tonight, they were just screeching into the night.

They'd perfected the werewolf howl, though, and I was sure they probably used it to keep away predators and people alike.

Unfortunately for them, I had someone special with me, and I would do anything to keep Jaden safe.

Even die.

Chapter 19

Fiona

I might have been an old witch, but I was not dumb.

That was the only way I'd been able to make it this long. My smarts, and my ability to think on me feet had saved me more times than I cared to count.

And now, those things were going to save me again.

It was probably going to be a long day of trying to figure out what we were supposed to do, so I went ahead and put the coffee on.

Eliza and Jasper had a lot of reading to do, and I needed to gather ingredients.

Tracking spells required several things: a collection of herbs, the right number of rabbit droppings, and an annoyingly large amount of luck.

Eliza's tracking spells weren't nearly as strong as Natasha's were, but I believed in us.

We were a team.

Like it or not, Eliza was stuck with both me and Jasper. The three of us were going to find Jaden because we all loved her. We all appreciated her.

And we all knew that Jaden was still a new witch.

Together, I believed we would be able to figure something out that would save Jaden and Stanley from whatever it was that they were dealing with.

Wherever they were, and whoever they were with, they wouldn't have to be alone forever.

We would help them.

They didn't even need to know where the help had come from. All they needed to know was that we would be there.

We would work until our magic ran out off if it meant saving our friends.

They didn't have to worry now or forever.

We were going to do whatever it took.

"It's been a long time since we've done this," Eliza murmured, looking up from a spell book.

"Tracked down your girlfriend's daughter?"

"Performed magic together," Eliza smiled.

Jasper, who was back in his human form and wearing a pair of sweatpants I kept around *just in case* he decided to be a man, rolled his eyes.

"It has been a long time," I agreed. "I've missed it."

"Me too."

Performing magic on your own was a lot of fun, but there was *nothing* that compared to doing spells or brewing potions with your best friends. Being able to create something that would change the world – or at least one person's world – was a powerful thing, and having companions who understood was...

Well, it was everything a witch could hope for.

Chapter 20

Stanley

"I'm sorry," I said to Jaden.

"For what?"

"I should have told you sooner than I was in trouble," I sighed. Really, I should have told her sooner that I was having a hard time with this hole "being a werewolf" thing.

I hadn't exactly woken up one day and planned to become a werewolf.

It wasn't like it was something you could really plan.

Oh, there were people who tried, sure.

I'd heard of people and been warned about them: humans who tried to lure werewolves into biting them.

The problem was that if you weren't careful, you could easily get tricked by either side.

If you were a human who wanted to be bitten by a vampire, for example, who was going to stop some vampire from promising you that they were good enough at the vampire life to make it happen?

Turning someone into a vampire wasn't something that just any vamp could do.

It took self-control, and it took patience, and there was a reason most of them didn't bother.

But vampires were sneaky creatures.

Maybe they'd even manage to convince you that they were a werewolf, too. Perhaps they'd tell you that you could become an *immortal* werewolf.

What happened when you found out you'd been tricked?

What happened when you realized that you weren't actually a vampire – just injured?

What happened when you finally grasped that you weren't an immortal werewolf – you were just cursed?

That was the problem with chasing after these big immortal dreams: you never knew what was going to actually happen to you.

People were sneaky, and they were tricky, and perhaps most of all, they wanted to believe in something.

People who wanted to be werewolves wanted to *feel* like there was something more to life than humanity.

So, someone might truly believe that they could be bitten and just turn into whatever creature was there, but the harsh reality was that unless a werewolf was in its werewolf form when it bit you, and unless the light of the full moon was shining on you, you weren't going to turn.

The moon *had* to be shining on you.

It had to be.

Otherwise, you were just some poor bloke who got attacked by a stranger in the dark.

That requirement for becoming a werewolf was the only real reason that I could think of that there weren't more werewolves in existence.

If you could just bite someone or scratch them and turn them into a werewolf, then the world would be overrun with chaos and ruin.

Not that werewolves were destructive in all the worst ways.

We weren't.

At least, not *all* of the time.

And we weren't monsters the way that, say, vampires were.

But we could get sloppy, and we could make mistakes, and yes, we could scratch or bite people if we got too worked up.

So, the fact that a werewolf had to be born beneath the full moon made sense to me. It was like nature had implemented this random rule for protecting the werewolf population.

There was a small limitation.

Besides, we didn't need more wolves.

If there had been more, then the world would be even more chaotic than it was now.

There would be more sadness.

More loss.

People would be mourning for their human lives that had been lost.

Because as much as I wanted to believe that werewolves could always control themselves and that we weren't as terrible as people said, the reality was that werewolves...

Well, werewolves were often hungry, vicious creatures.

And I was, too.

I was one of them.

When I was in my werewolf form, however, I wasn't out of control all of the time or even most of the time.

I wasn't completely wild.

I wasn't this broken, shell of a man.

It was just different.

I had a feeling that being turned into werewolf didn't make someone a murderer or a *monster*.

The werewolf virus didn't make you a killer.

What it did was enhance your personality.

I had been quiet and adventurous before everything happened, and I was still that way now, only a bit more so.

Other people, before being bit, had been mean and cruel.

Their werewolf senses only enhanced that.

Some people loved the idea that being a werewolf gave you an excuse to do what you wanted and to terrorize people if you needed to.

I wasn't that way.

Besides, I had something those other werewolves didn't.

I had the love of a good woman.

No matter what I was dealing with, I knew that Jaden wasn't going to leave me.

Only now, I wonder if I should have made her.

Maybe I should have tried to push her away.

Perhaps I should have done my best to make sure that she didn't come anywhere close to me.

Now that the end was here, it was starting to feel a little more damaged, a little more messed up.

And it was starting to make me think that perhaps the world wasn't the beautiful place that I really, really wanted it to be.

Jaden looked worried as she stared at me.

"Stanley, what's going on?"

I didn't know how much to tell her.

I didn't know just how deep I should dive into my reality.

I wanted to be honest, sure, but what I wanted even more than honesty was her to be safe.

I wanted her to be able to know that she was going to be fine.

But she couldn't be fine with me being hunted.

Chapter 21

Jaden

It was happening.

I could hear the werewolf outside of the hidden cave room, and I knew that he was close to finding our secret hideaway.

I shouldn't have cleared the spiders.

Perhaps if there were spiders, the person hunting us would have taken one look at the cave and just run in the other direction.

As it was, he didn't.

There were no spiders, and there was no reason for him to stay away, so he lurked out there in the main part of the cave.

His feet crunched on the ground as he stepped on a couple of leaves. When I got rid of the spiders, maybe I should have cleaned up the cave, too.

Wait a minute.

He was wearing *shoes*.

What kind of werewolf wore shoes?

Stanley seemed to notice it at the same time because he cocked his head, listening.

Okay, so whoever was out there might be hunting us, but he wasn't in his werewolf body. He was in his human form. That was good news, at least. It meant he'd be easier to fight.

Stanley and I sat together in the dim light of the little interior cavern, and we were silent as we listened.

Stanley probably thought we had more time, but we didn't. Once someone got your scent and started coming after you, that was it.

They never stopped.

This man wanted something from me. I wasn't sure whether it was my life or my hope or just my damn house.

Maybe it was just Stanley he was after, and that was a possibility, too, but I doubted it. Big bad villains never kept things simple. They went after you and the people you loved. They made it hurt.

So, I knew that this really was it.

This really was the moment where everything fell apart.

No matter what Stanley had done before, and no matter what he'd tried to hide, it was all coming to a head.

At this moment, his nemesis was coming to try to hurt me.

Hurt us.

Our entire world was falling apart and there was nothing we could do to stop it.

I didn't know any spells that could make us invisible. I didn't know a spell for protecting us from a literal werewolf.

Instead of studying defensive spells, I'd been working my ass off to try to *find* werewolves and figure out how to turn them human again.

I'd spent my time researching werewolf prevention spells.

I'd done everything in my power to protect him.

Still, it hadn't been enough.

I opened my mouth to say something to him. I wanted to promise him that everything was going to be okay.

I wanted to make him believe that no matter what, the two of us would find a way to survive.

Only, he shook his head.

He lifted a finger to his lips.

He didn't want me to say anything.

Didn't want me to accidentally reveal that the two of us were hiding here.

Because there was still a chance.

There was still a possibility that the person hunting us wasn't going to realize there was a second room in the cave.

There was still the slightest semblance of a chance.

Only...

Stanley reached for my hand and squeezed. I looked over at this man. I looked at the man that I loved, and I knew that he was going to do whatever it took to protect me.

And I realized that he was probably going to try to sacrifice himself.

I couldn't let him do that.

I couldn't let him try to throw himself in front of the monster for me.

Only, that was what Stanley always did.

Wasn't it?

He was always so worried about protecting me, but maybe this time he was the one who needed to be protected?

Maybe this time, he needed me.

There was a pause on the other side of the door.

I knew what it meant.

I knew this meant that our time was up, only I didn't want it to be.

Stanley couldn't fight against someone who had blown up my house.

He couldn't completely destroy everything

Besides, it wasn't a full moon.

The sun was coming up. It was the morning.

And the man was here.

Just as I heard him crawling under the little gab that would allow him into the secret room, I whispered the words that would put up a barrier ball. Pushing my hands outward, I pushed the barrier ball around the two of us.

Just as it wrapped around us, a man's head poked through. He looked up at us, blinking.

"Stanley?" The man seemed surprised. "What's going on?"

Chapter 22

Jasper

I sat in Fiona's kitchen, stirring the little cauldron that was in the center of the table.

"Shouldn't this be over an open fire?" I asked her.

She just shook her head at me.

"Stop trying to tell me about spells," she snapped.

"I wasn't trying to tell you about spells."

Only, I was.

I totally, completely was.

I didn't trust her.

Like, at all.

The biggest problem with Fiona was that she was far too concerned about being nosy and not nearly concerned enough about precision.

Her spells tended to come out sloppy and lumpy, and when she made things in her kitchen - whether it be a spell or, say, a pie - it was never the best product I'd seen in my life.

Most of the time, in fact, things were a little bit sloppy with most of the witches.

I understood that most of them had a lot on their mind, but it did bother me that in general, the witches of Which Village didn't seem particularly concerned about making sure that each of their spells hit the right things at the right time.

As a shapeshifter, I knew that precision was everything.

When I was trying to sneak around in my cat for, for example, I had to make sure that I didn't do anything that might be perceived as human.

Generally, I only had one chance at making sure that people thought I was who they thought.

If I wanted to reveal that I was a shapeshifter, it needed to be on my terms and my time.

If I wasn't careful, though, I might accidentally give myself away too early.

That was always a problem.

Now, I stirred the cauldron as Eliza and Fiona tossed in a number of different ingredients in varying amounts.

The one that surprised me most was the onions, actually.

Who knew that some spells could call for vegetables like onions?

To be it really seemed impossible and honestly, a little bit gross.

"Are you sure this is the right spell?"

"It's not going to be perfect," Eliza muttered. She looked up at me and our eyes locked. "No spell is perfect," she added, as though I didn't know.

"Natasha is the one who is really good at tracking spells."

"So, what's the big deal with this one?" I asked, gesturing at the pot. It was looking really, really nasty. "Is it even going to work?"

"We just need something that's going to get us going," Fiona told me.

"Something that will push is in the right direction," Eliza added.

"How much time do you think we have?"

"Not enough," they both said together.

"Who do you think is after her?"

That was probably an unfair question, but they both looked at me at the same time.

"Whoever it is, he's not going to be patient, and he's not going to give them a lot of time," Fiona said.

"We have to hurry," Eliza agreed. "The sooner we can get to them, the sooner we can make sure that they're safe."

"We need something more," Fiona stared at the bubbling mixture in front of me. How was it bubbling? There was no heat source. It was the strangest thing I'd never seen.

"What do we need?" I could run to the store.

"We need some of her hair."

I sighed. I knew without a doubt they were going to send me over to her house to sort through the rubble and bring back a hairbrush. It was always the cat who got stuck with jobs like this.

"I don't want to go," I snapped. I was tired and irritated. We'd been up all night long working on this stupid potion.

"Just go," Eliza said, using her most commanding voice. "As soon as you get her hairbrush, we'll have everything we need."

"And we'll be able to find her," Fiona added.

"I'll do it," I glared. "Not for you, though," I muttered.

I was doing this for one person, and one person only: Jaden.

The witch had never done me wrong before, so I owed her. I'd do this one thing for her, but that was it.

I peeled off my pants, walked to the kitchen door that led directly outside, and opened it. Then I shifted into my cat form and took off running. Making my way through the rubble of the burned-down house would be easy in this smaller body.

One hairbrush, coming up.

Chapter 23

Jaden

The man stared at us as though he was really confused to see the two of us just sitting in a cave. If I was being honest, he didn't exactly look scary or villainous at all.

This?

This was Stanley's nemesis?

I glanced over at my husband quickly, but his face was unreadable as he looked at the man. I could tell that Stanley knew him, but that was about the extent of what I could tell.

The strange man raised an eyebrow. He was still lying on his tummy halfway in and halfway out of the cave room.

"What's going on?"

I blinked, watching him.

What's going on?

That was his opener?

After all of that.

After everything.

After the two of us going through a nightmare of a situation, that was what he had?

What was going on?

Stanley and I were both silent as we looked at him.

"Excuse me?" Stanley asked.

"What's this?" The man slithered into the room, stood up, and looked at us. He stepped forward and stared at the boundary that was surrounding me and Stanley. It had a clear base, so when it poked it, the entire thing jiggled a little.

"Why is this here?"

Neither Stanley nor I seemed to know what to say to him.

I'd never had someone poke at a boundary I'd put up, nor had I ever had someone who seemed malicious end up being...

Curious.

Why was he curious?

I looked to Stanley, wondering what he was going to say, but he only shrugged.

It seemed as though he was as baffled as I was by this.

"Hey, you're Stanley, right? Long time, no see."

I looked once more to Stanley, who was glaring at the man.

"Leave us be, werewolf."

The werewolf dude looked a bit sullen.

"Hey, that's not cool, man," he said. "That's not very nice of you. You know, I don't come around calling you names, do I?"

Stanley shook his head. "Maybe you should," he glared at the man.

"Excuse me?"

"Maybe you should," Stanley sneered again.

It was weird. I felt like I was watching some sort of weird, shapeshifter showdown, only I didn't know who the good guy was, and who the bad guy was.

"Boys?" I asked. It was getting harder to keep the barrier up. If I could lower it, just for a little while, it would make things much easier on me.

"It's okay," Stanley said. "I know him."

"We go way back," the man grinned. Then his grin fell. "You look different, though."

"Because I'm not in my werewolf form," Stanley muttered. He looked to me, "he's only seen me when I'm a werewolf."

"That's why he asked if you were Stanley," I pointed out. Stanley nodded.

"You can lower the barrier, Jaden."

Chapter 24

Jaden

I wasn't particularly ready to lower my barrier spell, but Stanley seemed certain, and I didn't want to argue with him anymore.

So, I lowered it.

My spell dropped and the man near us seemed to be trying to decide whether to give Stanley a hug or a high-five. In the end, he chose to just awkwardly stand still and shove his hands in his pockets.

Thanks to the ball of light that I'd already cast but never put out, we could see him clearly. I realized suddenly that this was probably what had given us away.

He may have found the cave on his own, but the light shining out of the little interior room entrance must have been a real giveaway.

Internally, I chastised myself for being so careless.

"Careless" wasn't a good look for a witch.

"Joseph, why are you here?" Stanley asked, sighing. He shook his head.

So, this was the infamous Joseph.

This was the man who was going to destroy Stanley.

This was the man who wanted to ruin everything.

He looked...

Well, he honestly looked kind of harmless.

Joseph was slightly hunched-over because the cave was a bit short, and he was a little dusty. Honestly, he looked a little sad and thirsty.

Without him asking, I conjured up a little cup of ice water and handed it to him.

He seemed surprised but drank the whole cup quickly before handing it back.

What was I supposed to do with an empty paper cup? Creating things was easier than destroying them, at least for me, so I simply set the cup down next to all of Stanley's trail mix.

"Thank you," Joseph said.

"Of course."

I looked at Stanley and raised an eyebrow. I was waiting for him to explain what was going on, because nothing was making sense any longer.

This?

This was the big, bad man he'd been so worried about?

This was the werewolf that had been chasing him?

Then it hit me: this was the werewolf who had blown up my damn house. Irritation welled up within me, and I glared at the man before me. He shouldn't have done that.

"You destroyed my house," I snapped turning back to him.

"Oh," he looked sullen. "I'm sorry about that."

For some reason, I suddenly thought perhaps he hadn't meant to do it.

Was it possible that all of this had been a big misunderstanding?

I didn't want to believe that, but it was starting to look like it.

"What's the story there?" I asked.

"It was an accident," he said. "I mean, to be honest, it's nice to see Stanley, but really, I was looking for you. I didn't mean to destroy your house."

The damn werewolf looked crestfallen. I really wasn't sure how that had happened, except for the fact that he suddenly seemed like he needed nothing more in the world than a big hug and a real friend.

"Joseph, why are you here?" Stanley finally spoke up and had the balls to look irritated, if not outright annoyed.

"I need help," he said.

That caught me off-guard.

And once again, I realized that it seemed like everything I'd ever known or been taught about werewolves wasn't exactly true.

Was it?

I felt like I'd been taught that werewolves were rough around the edges.

Cruel.

Heartless.

Mean.

Vicious.

They were all of these terrible things, but the reality was that they weren't.

In reality, they were just people.

They were just people who were having a hard damn time, and that was enough for me.

Stanley seemed to feel the same way because instead of trying to fight Joseph, he just *looked* at him.

"What's going on, Joseph?"

"I heard about her," he pointed to me. "I know she knows about werewolves and how to fix us. I want the cure," he said firmly. "And I'm sorry, you know, about the house. I meant what I said. It was an accident."

"How do you accidentally blow up a house?" Stanley frowned.

"I was just trying to break in. There was a cat who scared me, and I dropped my fireworks." He shook his head.

"Fireworks?"

"I thought we'd celebrate after I talked to you," he whispered. "I thought you would help me."

"You wanted to talk to me, but you got scared by a cat," I repeated, trying to follow the story.

"Damn witchy cats and their powers. My stuff shouldn't have gone off just from being dropped, but I picked them up from a charm store, so they were probably hexed."

I sighed. There was only one scary cat in my neighborhood, and he wasn't really a cat at all.

"Jasper. That must have been Jasper."

Which meant the cat was aware that we were in trouble. If I had to guess, Fiona and Eliza were probably on their way here *right now*. Knowing there was backup coming was kind of a good feeling, not that we needed it any longer.

Joseph wasn't going to hurt us. Even if he wanted to, he didn't have a backpack anymore and it seemed like all of his fireworks had gone directly into my house.

Stanley looked from me to Joseph and back again.

"The cure," Joseph said again. "Please. I'm tired of this, Stanley. I'm ready to be free."

I was just about to open my mouth to tell him I was trying, that I was doing my best, and that I would make it happen literally as soon as I could when Stanley spoke up.

"I'm really sorry," he said. "But there is no cure."

Chapter 25

Stanley

"I should have told you before," I said to Jaden. I couldn't look at her for a long minute, but I could feel her staring at me.

I should have told her when I'd first arrived at the fair and I'd finally changed back to my human self.

Only, she'd been so excited and happy to see me, and I'd wanted that. I'd wanted to be with her. I might not have remembered her, but it was easy to see that I'd once loved her, and it was easy for me to know why.

"Then why didn't you?"

Jaden was mad. I could tell. It wasn't like we hadn't had fights before, but this felt different. This time, it was personal.

This time, I was clearly in the wrong, and I had clearly lied to her.

"Because I couldn't bring myself to be honest."

Because I couldn't bring myself to let her down when she'd hoped for this for so long.

Because she'd fought so hard.

Because she'd dreamed of getting her husband back.

And it was never going to happen.

"But my mother..." Jaden shook her head. I took her hands and held them tightly. Looked her in the eye. Pressed my lips together.

This was my wife.

This was the woman I had once planned to spend all of eternity with.

If I couldn't be honest with her, then I didn't deserve her.

"Your mother gave up," I told her quietly. It was something I'd never told anyone because it was such a terrible secret, and I was the only one who knew.

"What?"

"The night she died."

I remembered like it was just yesterday.

The moment was still bright and vivid in my mind, and there was nothing clogging that memory.

"You were there when her mom died?" Joseph asked. He raised an eyebrow. "No offense, man, but that's pretty messed up."

"Seriously?" I glared at the werewolf. "Not helping, man."

"All right, all right," he held up his hands and started to back away. "Sorry already. Sheesh."

His back hit the wall and he stayed there. Unless he wanted to drop to his belly and wiggle out through the tiny exit, he was stuck here with us.

Jaden, however, wasn't trying to escape. She was looking at me with a strange expression on her face, and it was all I could do to keep myself from just grabbing her and tugging her into my arms.

She'd been through so much, and now I was putting her through something else.

Something terrible.

And my heart hurt for her.

For us.

For this.

"What happened?"

I looked at her and shook my head.

"Stanley. What happened?"

"I wasn't there when she passed away," I told her. I'd heard the story. Heard the news. Read all about it.

She'd been murdered, mostly for her work trying to save the werewolves, but it was unfortunate because we couldn't be saved.

Besides, the potions were spilled.

Gone.

Destroyed.

"But your mother and I had been working together. We'd finally both come to the same conclusion, though."

"No cure?"

"No cure," I repeated. "We tried so many different things, and each time we tried a new potion, it would work for a day or two before the side effects would become unbearable."

"Side effects?" Joseph asked.

"Alicia and I realized that once you're bitten by a werewolf, the curse is *on* you. It's there to stay. It becomes a part of you. You can try to bury it, and you can try to tamp it down, but trying to cure it is what really makes people dangerous."

Jaden considered this.

"Tell me more."

"When someone tries to stop themselves from turning, they're basically forcing themselves into a little box. They're making it seem like nothing else matters except acting normal. Just like tamping down a normal emotion can lead to outbursts and fits, trying to cure someone's werewolf side does the same."

"How did you figure this out?"

I was embarrassed by my answer, but she had a right to know.

"Every time I tried a cure, I would attack someone."

"What?"

"Every time, Jaden."

Soon I couldn't deal with it anymore, and honestly, neither could Alicia. The two of us made a pact to stop trying, and she was going to help me reach out to Jaden.

Only, I couldn't *remember* Jaden.

I didn't know what she looked like.

Sounded like.

Acted like.

When I saw her again at the fair, I thought she was pretty, but I still didn't know her.

I didn't know anything about her.

"There's really no cure," she said slowly.

"There's really no cure," I agreed.

I sighed.

I'd done it.

I'd told her.

And the world hadn't ended.

Chapter 26

Jaden

Hours later, we were sitting outside of the cave with Eliza, Joseph, Fiona, and Jasper.

Jasper was in his cat form, and I had a feeling he planned to stay like that.

"I don't understand," Eliza said slowly. "When Jaden found you at the fair, you said you'd been stuck in your werewolf form for a long time."

"With the moon being hexed, I suddenly couldn't shift back any longer. While Alicia was alive, she'd cast temporary little cures on me so we could work together, but they never lasted long, and when they wore off, I'd attack people."

"Then after she died, you were just...stuck," I realized.

And my heart broke for Stanley a little bit.

He'd tried so damn hard, but he hadn't been able to find a cure for being a werewolf.

Then again, maybe having a werewolf for a husband wasn't the worst thing in the world.

We all sat around talking, trying to work out what our next steps were going to be – starting with the house repairs, of course – but eventually, everyone left except for me and Stanley, and I found myself sitting on the edge of the mountain with the man I loved.

"I'm sorry I didn't tell you sooner," he said.

"It doesn't matter."

"It does," he said. "It really, really does."

"No," I shook my head. "Stanley, this doesn't change anything for me."

"What are you talking about?"

"I still love you."

I still wanted to be with him.

*

Stanley

My heart swelled as I realized that she meant it. For so long, I'd been afraid that she wouldn't be able to accept me – the real me – but it seemed as though I was wrong, and she did.

She really, really did.

"Do you mean it?"

She nodded.

"For as long as I live, I'll be your bride. Will you be my werewolf lover?"

I raised an eyebrow.

"We can run together in the dark, Stanley. We can dance in the moonlight. It can be just the two of us forever and ever. What do you say?"

I looked at her and smiled. Then I said the only thing I possibly could.

"Forever and ever."

I'd finally found my hope.

And I'd found it with her.

THE END

Author

L.C. Mortimer loves books almost as much as she loves coffee. When she's not on a caffeine-induced writing spree, she can be found pole dancing, traveling, or playing with her pet hamster, Neko. Mortimer loves reading, playing video games, and spending time with her husband and kids. Please make sure to join her mailing list here.[1]

---

1. https://mailchi.mp/081b88e5b445/lcmortimer

Hybrid Academy: Year One

Do you love academy stories full of adventure and magic?
Check out Hybrid Academy: Year One.[1] It's on Amazon now!
You can also keep reading for a sneak peek!

"This isn't what I ordered." The tall man in the suit looked at the coffee and sneered. He thrust the cup back at me. A little bit sloshed over the side of the cup and onto the counter. "And you'd better clean that up."

Biting back irritation, I managed a smile.

"Of course. Anything else I can do for you?" I asked politely. Inside, I felt anything but polite. This guy was being a total jerk, as always. I knew for a fact that his coffee had been made perfectly. He just didn't like me because I couldn't do magic.

He wanted Maggie to make his drink.

"A free bagel couldn't hurt," the man said, jerking his head toward the display of blueberry bagels.

"I'll have to get my manager's permission," I said. "Please wait just a moment."

I scurried to the back of the café and knocked on the door to the office.

"Come in."

I yanked the door open and peered inside. Tony was sitting at his desk with his ankles crossed over the top. He looked bored out of his mind.

"What do you want, Maxine?" He asked.

---

1. *https://www.amazon.com/Hybrid-Academy-Year-L-C-Mortimer-ebook/dp/ B07SR5CTYB*

"It's Max," I said. "Not Maxine. And there's a customer who wants a free bagel."

"We don't give out bagels for free," Tony said with a yawn. He was obviously bored. He was always bored at the café.

"I know, but he said that his drink was wrong and he wants to be compensated with free food."

Tony glared at me and got up with a huff. He acted like it was my fault that he was the manager of the café or that he had to leave the safety of his office to come do his actual job. Whatever. I'd been dealing with Tony ever since I started working at the café. He was neither a good boss nor a team player, so I tried to stay as far away from him as possible. Besides, something about Tony made me uncomfortable, and I couldn't quite pinpoint why.

"Is there a problem, Lionel?" Tony asked the tall man.

"Yeah, your em-ploy-ee," he dragged the word out sarcastically. "Messed up my drink. I asked her nicely if she could fix it."

"Not a problem," Tony said. He jerked his head toward one of my coworkers. "Maggie, make Lionel a new drink."

Maggie shot me a nasty look but nodded and started the drink. The café wasn't busy and the drink wasn't complicated, so I wasn't sure what the big deal was. Actually, I had the distinct feeling that Lionel's original drink had been just fine, but that he wanted a bagel out of the deal.

Correction: he wanted a *free* bagel.

Tony and Lionel sat and chatted while Maggie made the drink. I cleaned up the spill on the counter before starting to check our inventory. I wasn't a magic user, so I couldn't just summon cups whenever we ran out of something we needed. Instead, I'd have to trot back to the stockroom, find what we needed, and carry it back. It was kind of a drag for everyone, which was just another reason nobody liked me.

By the time I left work that day, I was tired, exhausted, and spent.

And I knew my grandmother was going to be beyond pissed that I was late.

*

I ran up the steps to the little log cabin where I lived with my Grandmother. My heart was pounding, racing, and I silently begged it to stop. *Slow down*. It needed to chill out, to be honest. Overreacting never turned out well for anyone, least of all me.

I smelled sweaty and I was tired: both signs that I left work much later than I should have. I didn't want her to give me a hard time about it. Mémère had enough to worry about. She didn't need to be concerned that my boss still wasn't letting me leave on time or that my customers were constantly giving me a hard time.

That's the price I paid to work at a café in Brooksville.

Nobody liked me because I was poor, and an orphan, and I couldn't do magic.

All of those elements combined to make me one of the most disliked people in town. Despite trying to have a charming personality and showing kindness to the people around me, I somehow still managed to catch the eye of every magic-user within shouting distance, and not in a good way.

I glanced down at my work clothes. My once-white blouse was now splattered with coffee, no thanks to Maggie and Justine for their "assistance" at work. My jeans had fared just as poorly. They had a few new stains, a new tear, and smelled slightly questionable. I sighed. Mémère was definitely going to notice something was wrong.

I hated to make her worry.

I hated to make her sad.

She worked so hard to raise me, to take care of me, that the idea of letting her down again filled me with stress and anxiety. I wished for the millionth time that I could use magic. I wished that I had a wand, that I knew spells, or that I had, you know, *powers*. I wished that I could whisper a few carefully practiced words and somehow whip up an appearance she could be proud of.

But I couldn't.

In my case, practice hadn't made perfect.

I stared at the front door of our home for a long minute. My breathing finally began to stabilize and I began to feel like everything was going to be okay. Maybe it would. Maybe everything would be fine. One bad day at work wouldn't kill me.

A hundred bad days at work wouldn't kill me.

Besides, I owed Mémère *everything*. Without her, I wouldn't exist. I would have died when my parents did. I would have been killed or lost or starved. No one else in this place was about to take in a little orphan kid who couldn't do spells. Nobody. Yet my grandmother was ready.

My grandmother was brave.

I reached for the door and pressed my hand against it, but I didn't turn the knob. Not yet. I needed a few more minutes to be alone with my thoughts, to focus on the fact that today had been the worst day yet. Today seemed different somehow. Part of me thought that after awhile, things at work would get easier. I thought that they'd improve and that I would finally begin to connect with people who understood me.

I was so wrong.

I'm not understood now, just like I wasn't understood before.

A tear slid down my cheek and I brushed it away. I look around wildly, like someone could see me, even though I was completely alone.

"I know you're out there," I heard her voice through the door. "Come on in, love. I won't bite."

I gulped.

Yeah, my grandmother definitely knew something was up. She didn't want me working in town, anyway, but I had convinced her that I needed to. The reality was that I knew she didn't have a lot of money and I felt bad for not contributing to our family. The café didn't bring in a lot of money, but I was finished with school and wasn't really doing anything else with my time.

There weren't a lot of job prospects in Brookville, but the café was something. It enabled me to make some money, spend time socializing, and get to know people who lived near me. It meant I could be around other people, for once. It meant I could explore the world, if only just a little.

The front door opened before I could turn the knob, and there stood my grandmother: tall, lean, and silvery.

Fierce.

My grandma was fierce.

Everything about her screamed *strong*. She was taller than me, which was sometimes hard for me to grasp since at 5'7", I wasn't a tiny girl. Although she was getting older, she still had strong muscles that were clearly defined. Whether it was from being a witch or from years of exercise and hard work, I wasn't sure. I just knew that my grandma wasn't the type of person anyone messed with.

Not if they knew what was good for them.

"You're late," she said simply, but she glared when she did. Her eyes narrowed a little: not too much. She didn't quite look *mad*. It was more like, a cautious sort of look, as though she was waiting for me to say something first. I knew exactly what she wanted from me. She wanted me to admit that working in the shop was a bad choice and that I was ready to stay home with her.

After all, even if I couldn't use magic, I could still learn about it, and my grandmother loved it when I studied.

"Not by much," I responded, but I knew instantly it was the wrong thing to say. My grandmother didn't yell at me or raise her voice. She never had. We didn't have that kind of relationship. Besides, disappointment was so much worse than yelling, anyway. If I wanted to trick Gram, I should have acted stupid. I should have pretended like I didn't know just how late it was. Then I could have pretended that I was lollygagging or chatting with someone and just completely lost track of the time.

My answer let her know that I knew I was late, and that there was a reason for it.

"What happened?" She said gently. Her eyes softened when she looked at me. Mr. Boo, my familiar, came out of the cabin and rubbed against my legs. I reached down and picked up the fat, black-and-white cat and held him in my arms for a minute. Somehow, Boo always managed to calm my racing heart when I felt stressed. I might not do magic, but Grams had given him to me just the same.

"Every witch should have a familiar," she had told me that day. Boo had been a full-grown cat already. No one knew exactly how old he was or where he'd come from, but Gram had chosen him and he turned out to be just as special as she thought he would.

"It's nothing, Mémère," I told her. "I just got caught up at work."

"Did you get busy at work, Maxine, or did someone make you stay late out of spite?" She didn't ask it in an accusing way, but I knew what she was thinking. Mémère didn't like me working for my boss. She didn't understand why I wanted to work or why I thought it was important that I have a job of some sort.

Any sort.

In her mind, my time would be better spent helping out on the property, working in the yard, or memorizing spells from the big, heavy book she kept on the kitchen table. The pages were worn with years of use, but Grams told me every day how important those spells were.

Not that I'd ever use them.

The little cabin we lived in was surrounded by a wide yard and then trees for as far as the eye could see. Our driveway itself was almost a mile long. That's how hidden away we were. Unless someone was looking for us specifically, they'd never find us. We didn't even get mail at the house. Everything went to a post office box in town that one of us would check on a weekly basis.

Mémère and I were isolated, and she worried about me.

"You know Tony likes to have me stay late sometimes," I finally said. It wasn't a lie, but it was sort of a half-truth. I didn't know if Tony actually liked having me stay or if he just liked having me miserable. Did I get paid for staying late? Yeah. Of course. This wasn't some sort of illegal café. That said, it was still a nightmare working late after I'd already been on my feet for an eight-hour shift.

My grandmother sighed and shook her head.

"This man is no good for you," she said.

"He's not my man," I pointed out. I didn't date. Mémère knew that. A lot of things kept me from relationships and one of the biggest reasons was that I didn't want to date a magic user. It wasn't my thing. I couldn't use magic. I had never been able to get even the simplest spell to work. My grandmother did her best to train me in the ways of her people, but somehow, I'd just never managed to pick things up.

If it bothered her, she was kind enough not to tell me.

Still, I didn't want to date someone who could use magic. Part of it was a safety thing. Self-preservation was important and I didn't want to be in a relationship with someone who might do a love spell on me. I just hated the idea of not knowing what was going on.

I hated the idea that someone might take advantage of me.

"He's still cruel," Mémère said. She shook her head. She was disappointed. In me? In the situation? I wasn't sure, but I nodded in agreement and moved past her and into the house. I dropped my bag on the living room sofa and walked into the attached kitchen. The book with Mémère's spells, as always, was spread out in the center of the table. Gram had been working on spells this afternoon. Herbs and pots and potions and bottles were on every flat surface in the room.

"What were you working on?" I asked her, but she only shook her head gently. Grams never liked to talk about the spells she was doing. I didn't really understand why it had to be a secret. She wanted me to trust her, but there were so many things she wouldn't reveal to me.

"Are you hungry?" Mémère asked, and I knew there was to be no discussion on what she was trying to do with her spell book. It didn't make sense to me. Sometimes it seemed like she had just as many secrets as Mom and Dad.

"I ate at work," I lied. She looked at me carefully. Was she trying to see if I was lying? I totally was, but this time, there was no way for her to tell. Not unless she used some sort of truth serum on me. I wouldn't put it past her, but this wasn't something I was ready to talk about today. Not with Grams.

"If you change your mind..." Her voice trailed off and I nodded.

"Don't worry. I'm 19, Grams. I'm old enough to make myself something to eat."

I kissed her softly on the cheek and turned to the little staircase that led upstairs. Our home was very cozy, but it was also very small. The second floor of the cabin had only two little bedrooms and a tiny bathroom with a sink, a toilet, and a shower. I went up the stairs and sat at the very top for a minute. I listened to see if I could figure out what Gram was up to.

I heard her bustling around in the kitchen for awhile, touching things and whispering, but she was so quiet that I couldn't make out the words. When Boo came up the narrow staircase and rubbed against my legs, I reached for him and pet him softly. Instantly, he started to purr.

"At least I have you," I whispered, and I pulled him into my lap. I held Boo for a long time. Then I stood up and carried him into my bedroom and shut the door behind me. I locked the door. It didn't matter. If Gram needed to come in, she could cast a spell and be in my space in like, two seconds.

But the lock made me feel like I was tucking myself away from everything: my boss, my job, my lack of friends. I used it because it gave me a little bit of security I wouldn't otherwise have. I lay on my bed and looked at the ceiling.

"What am I going to do, Boo?"

He purred and plopped his fat body onto my tummy. I pet him as I looked up at the white popcorn finish on the ceiling. I imagined that I was back home – at my real home – with my mom and dad. They'd been gone for years. Sometimes it felt like forever. I missed them still.

People always said that life got better. They said things like "time heals all wounds" and "one day, it won't hurt so bad," but that wasn't true, was it? Things still hurt. I still missed the way my mom sang songs while she cooked spaghetti and the way my dad laughed as he danced in the kitchen with her. I missed the way they read me bedtime stories and how they used to count the stars with me. I missed everything about them.

Mémère was a wonderful person. She was kind and brave and I was so incredibly lucky to have her, but...

But she wasn't my mom.

And sometimes I just wanted my mom.

Finally, I got up and started getting ready for bed. I went into the bathroom and brushed my teeth and my hair. Then I came back, brushed Boo, and picked out my outfit for the next day. I double checked my work schedule and figured out what time I needed to get up in order to make it in for my shift. Then I closed my eyes.

I tried to fall asleep, but I laid in bed thinking for what seemed like hours.

I heard a crash, and Mémère let out a string of swear words. She would be working late into the night, I guessed, and I had no idea what she was doing down there.

What was so important that she couldn't tell me about it?

And why did I have the feeling it wasn't anything good?

Want to keep reading? Check out Hybrid Academy: Year One.[2]

---

2. *https://www.amazon.com/Hybrid-Academy-Year-L-C-Mortimer-ebook/dp/ B07SR5CTYB*

Don't miss out!

Visit the website below and you can sign up to receive emails whenever L.C. Mortimer publishes a new book. There's no charge and no obligation.

https://books2read.com/r/B-A-XYLC-SFIZB

Connecting independent readers to independent writers.

Also by L.C. Mortimer

Which Village
Don't Cry Over Spilled Potions

Standalone
Swords of Darkness
Just Another Day in the Zombie Apocalypse
The Death of Planet 86